The Hunger Bone

The Hunger Bone

ROCK & ROLL STORIES

Debra Marquart

Headwaters 2
2001

First edition
Library of Congress Control Number: 00-105589
ISBN: 0-89823-209-0
Book design and typesetting by Percolator
Printed in Canada

New Rivers Press is a nonprofit literary press dedicated to publishing
emerging writers.

The publication of *The Hunger Bone* has been made possible by a gener-
ous grant provided by the Minnesota State Arts Board, through an appro-
priation by the Minnesota State Legislature. In addition, this activity is
supported by a grant from the National Endowment for the Arts.

Additional support has been provided by the General Mills Foundation, the
McKnight Foundation, the Star Tribune Foundation, and the contributing
members of New Rivers Press.

NATIONAL
ENDOWMENT
FOR THE
A R T S

New Rivers Press
420 North Fifth Street Suite 1180
Minneapolis, MN 55401

www.newriverspress.org

for the players, especially Peter

In the beginning there was a river. The river became a road, and the road branched out to the whole world. And because the road was once a river, it was always hungry.

BEN OKRI, *THE FAMISHED ROAD*

Contents

THREE-MILE LIMIT

We pulled into our guitar player's driveway at first light. The birds were chattering in the linden tree next to the driveway. It was the loudest noise I'd heard so early in the morning that wasn't leftover noise from the night before. Troy lived on the edge of town in a new development full of winding streets and cul-de-sacs with names like Shady Acres and Lake View, even though there wasn't a lake for thirty miles.

Joey put the van in park and pulled the emergency brake. He honked the horn, three sets of triplets—*tri-pa-let, tri-pa-let, tri-pa-let*. Drummers. Then he held it down, one long foghorn blow.

The house was a two-story white clapboard with a bay window and a small front porch with wind chimes and bentwood rockers. Arrangements of pink and blue petunias bloomed beside the steps. Around the side were sprays of yellow rose bushes. I mean, the place was landscaped. Beds of wood chips lay scattered around the base of trees and bushes.

"Susan's really settling in," Joey said from behind the wheel, looking at the scene as if watching film develop.

"The nesting urge," I said. Susan was our guitar player's new wife. In the two years we'd played with Troy, his interests had been guitar, guitar, and more guitar. Since Susan, it was china patterns, fabric swatches, and lead crystal. He had to be consulted on every decision, and we had to hear every painful detail afterward. As the only woman in the band, it should have been my job to like Susan, but even I wasn't about to.

We sat in the van and listened to the birds rioting in the linden tree. Hundreds of them hopped from branch to branch like it was a house party. A few lifted off in small groups and looped through the air in tight formation, then circled back. The treetop was black with birds. The branches shook. The leaves twisted in the air and floated to the ground.

"Damn grackles," Johnston, our bass player, said from the backseat. His voice was low and grouchy with morning. He had crawled into the van twenty blocks away on Culpepper and would stay under the blanket until noon.

"I think they're starlings," I said.

"Whatever," Johnston mumbled. By nighttime, his friends José or Jack would undo the hard knot of his voice, but that bad mood—nothing to be done for it. We'd carried it with us from state to state for over a year.

We sat in Troy's driveway and waited. One song ended on the radio, a few commercials played. The crass unfunny banter of the DJ came and went, then another song began.

"Don't make me come in there and get you," Joey said, sounding like someone's dad. His nose had a bump and a crook in it, like it had been broken and healed wrong. His hair hung down his neck and shoulders in shaggy layers. A tarnished skull-and-crossbones earring dangled from his right lobe.

The circles under his eyes were dark as bruises. I wondered if he'd slept at all during our week off. It was never a good idea to cancel a gig and leave the guys alone with too much time and not enough money. Musicians are like fruit. They go bad quickly.

The week before at Spanky's, my throat started out low and froggy on Monday, then went down to five hoarse notes by Tuesday. By Wednesday, nothing—just a dry, catgut whisper. Even Spanky's hot buttered rums couldn't put the resin back. Finally we gave up and drove five hundred miles home with two nights' pay. I spent the rest of the week in bed, drinking hot tea and watching soap operas.

If you think your life is bad, just check out daytime television: obsession, depression, and demon possession; husbands who cheat; brothers who embezzle; shadowy criminal figures who bury you alive in underground caverns equipped with drinking straws and tiny video cameras so that they can better torture you. After a week of watching daytime, I was happy to be sitting in any driveway on Monday morning on the way to a gig.

"C'mon, pretty boy," Johnston yelled out the window. Surely we spent half our lives waiting for Troy.

Joey slumped over the wheel and pressed his forehead into the horn. He banged his head against the steering wheel. Little barking honks followed. Then he pressed down hard on the horn with his forehead and held it for an eight-count. The sound was monstrous in the early morning quiet. It bounced off the garage and rang through the still neighborhood.

"Quiet, he's a homeowner now." I nudged Joey, and we both started to laugh. With the money we made each week—about seventy-five bucks apiece after we covered agency fees, gas, motel expenses, and equipment payments—we were all surprised that any of us could end up owning a home, especially our can-I-borrow-five-bucks Troy owning a house in a place called Pleasant Hills, even if there were no hills to recommend it.

Susan had money, we found out after they were married. Her father had inherited gobs of farmland on the north side of town where the city was expanding. You wouldn't have known it from her silver toe rings and torn jeans when she first came out to see us, winking at Troy like any barfly and drinking Tequila Sunrises with cherry swirls of grenadine. She told me later she was slumming with her girlfriends the night she stumbled into the Zodiac, a biker bar we played that was best known for its gleaming rows of Harleys parked at a slant out front, and its bimonthly stabbings and shootings.

Just as Joey was about to get out of the van and rap on the front door, Troy's front light came on. The fixture glowed like a candle inside a golden globe. The sun was already up, so it wasn't much use. The screen door opened a crack, and Troy's hand appeared, his wide palm raised in the air like a traffic cop. He looked like he was struggling to get out the door but was being held by some force within. Joey took one last drag on his cigarette, then flicked it out the window. The cherry broke apart and skidded down the driveway.

"Oh, honey," Johnston growled from the back and fell on his pillow in a mad embrace. "Don't leave me now."

"Yeah, baby, I'll miss you too," Joey said, and kicked his big black boot into the van door, which fell open with a crunch of metal meeting metal. It sounded like something inside coming unhinged. The door made that sound ever since last year when a drunk fan rammed into us with her vintage Mustang behind the Rusty Nail. The name of our band was Everything Goes, and usually everything did. But sometimes things went wrong.

The front door of the house opened wider and Troy looked out, squinting in the early morning light. He pulled on a pair of black wraparounds and stepped onto the front stoop. He must have rolled out of bed at our first honk. He was wearing jeans and a pair of undone boots, the laces pulling wide at his ankles.

He stood on the front steps and pulled on his shirt. The ripples of his stomach showed tan against the denim. I noticed these things about him. Let's just say I noticed.

We were lucky to have Troy in the band. Never mind his playing, just the way he looked brought people out to see us. He had long, guitar-player legs, long dark hair, and those lush, sad-boy eyelashes that inspired women to want to have a man's baby. He had smooth olive skin and jutting cheekbones that cast gorgeous shadows under the stage lights. Behind the sunglasses, his eyes were deep set and dark as obsidian. They gave off a silvery hematite sheen. If you looked close enough, you could see your reflection in them.

Most people woke up with ratty bed hair and funky goo lodged in the corners of their eyes, but not Troy. In the two years since he started playing with us, I'd seen him get out of bed and look like he could walk into a Calvin Klein ad. Sometimes I'd been the one to wake him—to sit by his bed shaking him to tell him it was time to go—and he would sit up in the sheets, his lips full from sleep. He'd rub his face, brush his hands through his hair, and look better than ninety-five percent of the people in the world looked on their best day.

Now fully dressed, Troy yawned and motioned for us to wait one more minute, then stepped inside the front door to pick up his gear. He returned with two long black guitar cases under his right arm and Susan tucked in the crook of his left arm. She was laughing. She waved, and I waved back. She was dressed in oversized flannel pajamas and wool slip-ons. She looked straight from bed, too, but still sunny and beautiful with her long straight blond hair and no makeup. They kissed on the stoop.

"Oh, baby, be good," Johnston murmured in the backseat.

"You be good, too, baby," I whispered in return.

Then Troy stepped backward down the three stairs, Susan hanging on with both arms. The screen door snapped shut behind her with a loud clank, and all the birds lifted from the linden's branches. Hundreds of sleek black bodies flew from the tree and scattered in all directions. Off to different yards and different trees.

It's hard to say how it started, exactly, for me with Troy. I still remember the first moment I saw him in the rented storage garage where we practiced, right off of NP Avenue behind the railroad tracks. We were auditioning new guitar players because our old guitarist, Jimmy B., had disappeared.

The whole time we played with Jimmy B., he was AWOL from the army, which made him generally hard to locate when we needed him. If we called his house, his mother would say, "Jimmy, no, I haven't seen him," almost like she wasn't quite sure who Jimmy B. was. Until we would say, "It's us, Mrs. Barnes, the band." Then she would turn the receiver away and scream, "Jimmy, it's for you."

But one weekend we played in Detroit Lakes, a resort town that triples its population in the summer—and you can imagine how many blonds in french cuts that makes. And when it was time to go home, we couldn't find Jimmy. When Monday came, we couldn't find Jimmy, then the next weekend came and we still couldn't find him. Jimmy B. had become AWOL, even from us.

So that's how we found Troy, through an ad in the paper. He was one of about twenty guys to audition. There were country guys with big clunky hollow-bodies, and metal guys with flying Vs and hundred-watt Marshall stacks. There was a guy who hadn't taken his guitar out of the case since high school, but his wife had said, "Go for it."

Our keyboard player at the time tried to get him in tune, playing the notes—E-E-E, A-A-A, and so on—and signaling the guy, who was tightening and loosening his tuning pegs with no sense of sharpness or flatness. Our keyboard player kept screaming, "Up, up, bring it up." It took all of twenty minutes just to get his six strings tuned, so the guy never did get to audition. Then there was the Holy Roller who consulted his pastor before coming over. He told us that his pastor had counseled him, about the possibility of playing in bars, "Well, Hal, you gotta go where the sinners are."

So by the time Troy walked in with his blond Strat and his modest thirty-watt practice amp, and his slow tasty licks, we were ready for him. And he was one of those guys—he was like a bull's-eye. As soon as you met him you were trying to figure out where you knew him from. For a long time, I thought we'd met before. I didn't remember his face, but I knew his voice, which was a low rumble in his chest, a voice full of old bones and dust. And I knew his hands, those wide palms and long fingers that sustained my voice each night, playing flawless chords and riffs and solos on the neck of his guitar—the same hands I tried to place my body in the path of whenever possible the first year we played together.

That night of the auditions, after all the guitar players cleared their equipment away, the band closed the door of the practice garage and voted on who would be our next guitar player. We did it on paper, so no one could sway someone else's vote. It's a solemn decision, choosing a band member. You'll be broke and tired and stuck in small spaces with this person for hundreds of hours. Every piece of paper had Troy's name on it, except for one which, as a joke, had a vote for Hal the Holy Roller and his liberal-minded pastor.

Getting out of town is always the hardest part. Even though there are only five of us—Troy, Joey, Johnston, me, and our soundman, Tom, whom everybody calls Tommy Boy—we can still drive up and down the backstreets all morning, lingering in driveways, loading gear. Later there will be stops at the coffee place, the gas station, then the rest area.

In order to be in a band, you have to be able to do something like sing or play an instrument or run sound or lights, but the most important skill, the one that's absolutely essential, is knowing how to wait. You must be able to wait for everyone else's hunger to be satisfied, for the two minutes it takes to nuke a burrito bomb, for the ten minutes it takes to smoke a joint.

You must wait for bladders to be relieved, and for the little click of the lever that tells you the gas tank is filled. While you wait, fuses will be replaced, strings changed, and the roll of duct tape will be found. You must wait for drunks to be removed, for equipment to be packed, and for guitar players to go inside the house one last time to say good-bye to their wives.

Behind the van in Troy's driveway, Joey wrestled the guitars and amp into the small space left between the wheel wells. The van lurched and swayed with his pushing. I sat in the front of the van on the ten-gallon cooler we kept between the bucket seats. I was good at this waiting because I knew what rewards would come to me. By tomorrow night, I would be in another part of the country, screaming my lungs out at a place called the Cat's Paw. Not exactly the Fillmore, but consider the alternatives—I could have been in some kitchen in Kansas sweeping the linoleum and spooning strained carrots into the mouth of a fat-faced baby. By some miracle, I was not.

Behind the van, Joey gave one final tug on the equipment and slammed the double doors shut. A blast of air spread through the van.

"Don't wake me up until we see mountains," Johnston

said and fell back in the bunk. We had all day to make it to Bozeman. We'd probably get there around ten that night, check into a motel, and sleep. The next day we'd set up the equipment, sound-check, and play that night.

Now Troy came out of his front door carrying his suitcase. He walked down the driveway and headed for the van. I braced myself. The first few minutes around him were always the hardest. I put my feet up on the engine hump and hugged my knees.

Troy pulled open the passenger door and threw his suitcase in the back of the van. "Hey, Ninj," he said to me. He called me that, *Ninj*, short for Ninja, instead of my real name, Nina, which was just fine with me. It was my grandmother's name, and it didn't seem right in this part of the world. Did he also know I practiced the art of invisibility?

"Hey," I said back.

Troy slid into the front passenger seat and pulled the van door shut. This is the way we usually traveled: with Johnston and Tommy Boy sleeping in the back of the van, which had been stripped down and outfitted with a couch and some bunks; and Joey, me, and Troy rotating across the two front seats and the cooler. I liked to sit on the cooler, even though it didn't have a backrest, because I wanted to keep Troy on my right side.

I had two different profiles. On the left, my nose turned up in a slight pug and my cheekbone flared wide, making me look like everybody's cute kid sister. But on the right side, my nose ran straighter, my jawline stronger, and my cheekbone followed a stricter angle with my face, only breaking into a slight flare at the top. It made me look aloof, like a woman who could demand things and expect to get them.

"How's the pipes?" Troy smiled and motioned toward my throat. He reached his hand out and rested his palm on my adam's apple. His fingers wound around my neck and stayed there for a moment like he was checking my pulse. His hand felt cool and dry against my skin. He looked at me a little harder now. He was staring—I could see behind his sunglasses—at my hair, which I had dyed the deepest jet-blue-black I could find during our week off.

Should there be a three-day waiting period on over-the-counter hair dye? Even as I stood in the beauty section in front of all the hair products, I had wondered this. My natural color was chestnut brown. People told me it was warm. I thought it was boring. I liked the way my new hair color brought things into focus, clarified the lines around my face, made me stand out like a major figure in a minor painting.

"The voice is back," I whispered. "It's a little rough."

He drew his hand away, and I trilled out a supersonic *eeeeh*, then swooped down to my lowest note, *oooh*. This was the sound I made first thing every morning to see what kind of damage my voice had sustained the night before. It was a test pattern, like the color spectrum you see on TV after hours. If I could get from the top to the bottom of the trill without breaking, I knew I could make any noise I wanted to onstage.

"Sounds like old Ironsides is back in the harbor," Johnston said.

"We're not at Livingston yet," I yelled back, putting some grit on my voice.

Joey opened the front door and hopped into the driver's

seat, the van rocking with his weight. "Let's haul," he said, and turned the key. He stepped on the clutch and jammed the transmission into reverse.

Just then the front door of Troy's house opened and Susan came running down the driveway. She had thrown a gray flannel robe over her pajamas. She flashed an apologetic smile and waved for us to stop. In her right hand, she balanced a white paper plate.

"Aw, she shouldn't a oughta," Johnston said.

"Hi, guys." Susan smiled and circled around to Troy's side. "Honey," she whispered, "you forgot your breakfast." She pressed the Chinet plate through the window. On it was the most carefully prepared arrangement of french toast I'd ever seen—thick slices of homemade bread slathered in butter, a sprig of mint for garnish, and fresh blueberries swimming in an ocean of warm syrup.

"Yeah, honey," Johnston growled, "you forgot your breakfast." The smell of cinnamon and vanilla filled the van.

"Shut up, you guys." Susan laughed. She pulled Troy to her through the window and held his face in her hands as they kissed. It was a beautiful thing to see.

"Uh," Joey said, letting out the clutch. "Gotta book." Susan stepped back and waved. The van rolled down the driveway. We waved back.

Troy let out one long breath and rolled up the window. He balanced the plate of french toast in his left hand until we rounded the corner. Then he handed it back to Johnston, who would wolf it down, we knew, by the city limits.

"Five days is way too long to be home," Joey mumbled. "Too many entanglements."

"Tell me about it," Troy said, then he looked at me like it was all my fault for losing my voice. "Let's not do that again."

Next we picked up Tommy Boy, who lived on the west side of town in the basement of his mother's house, and we talked in the front yard with his mom for a while. After that we stopped for gas.

I was standing beside the van, minding the pump. This was my job because the smell of gasoline was sweet to me, comfortable as the smell of baking bread. The pump churned, and I breathed it in. I had a little moment of confluence then—the numbers spinning on the dial clicked out a complicated polyrhythm, and I noticed a delivery truck in the alley had its flashers going in unison with the gas pump's clicking. Then a train went by, and the whistle, I swear, blew in perfect syncopation.

All these things coming together made me feel happy, like the universe was arranging itself in some amazing order. Was my new black hair improving my mood? My blood pumped warm inside my chest; my skin glowed in the rearview mirror. Was it his closeness? Some chemical that made the reds redder and the sweets sweeter?

The gas pump clicked off, breaking the rhythm, and then I saw it was just one of those cool, overcast mornings that felt empty and too silent. I went into the station and paid for the gas. Troy held the door open, trailing behind me with a fistful of beef jerky. I don't know how we would have made it from one city to another without Uncle Milo's Secret Cajun Recipe.

"Thanks, jerky boy," I said to Troy. That's what we all

called each other: *Hey, jerky boy, get off my bed; Gimme some money, jerky boy.* Driving to gigs, we ate so much jerky we considered changing our name to the Jerky Band. We had high hopes for endorsements. "Not only are we the spokesmen, we are the company's best customers."

Troy followed me through the parking lot. "So what did you do to yourself?" he said, taking up a long strand of my new black hair. It looked just right, I thought, flowing like ink through his hands. I kept moving. He had his sunglasses off, and it was hard to look him in the eyes.

"Never leave me alone for five days without a voice," I said and pulled away. The strands slipped from his hands like black silk.

"Well, I was worried about you, Ninj," he said, following me to the van. And I wondered what he meant by that—worried like a dad, like a brother, like a lover? Or worried like another person in the band who depended on my voice for his livelihood?

That's the way our conversations always went. We'd be talking about music, then we'd be talking about how playing music was like having an orgasm, then we'd be talking about having an orgasm. And I'd walk away wondering what we'd just talked about. Nothing of what we understood about each other was known through words or ever spoken.

But how can I explain that I knew every inch of him, knew the warmth of his breath close to my face, how it might feel to run my palm in one smooth stroke down his chest. I had imagined the weight of him, knew how his hands would feel cupped under me, how my body would come unhinged beneath him.

"And how's the happy homeowner life?" I said to Troy. I opened the door of the van and crawled in.

"Did you spend the weekend raking leaves?" Johnston asked. After a few days off, we usually got a full accounting of his household activities. The rest of us would talk about cigarettes and Scotch, Muddy Waters and Deep Purple, and Troy would talk about trash compactors and weed whackers.

"Don't ask," he said, staring at the traffic that passed by the station. Joey was washing the windshield. We sat in silence and watched him scrub the bugs off, then dip the squeegee and plow clean rows on the glass.

There was one time, before he married Susan, when I tried to tell Troy everything—one time when I turned to him in all seriousness and said, "I need to talk to you about something." We were alone in the van, and he nodded quickly as if he knew, too, that we needed to talk, like maybe he'd wanted to say the same thing.

And when we loaded into the motel that night, he'd looked back in my direction and said, "Room 343?" as if to register where he could find me, and said, "I'll call you later." When I got back to the room, I unpacked and took a bath and waited for the phone to ring, but it never did. Not at ten o'clock or eleven, or at twelve, when I disconnected the phone because the silence of an unplugged phone was better than the silence of a phone that was not about to ring.

And the next morning at breakfast, and the next afternoon setting up equipment, even when we were alone, there was no acknowledgment of something left undone—no "Gee, I got tied up" or "Sorry, the guys wanted to go out for pizza." And from me there was no "Where were you?" or

"Why didn't you call?" because I decided long ago I was not that kind of woman.

In the last year, I'd spent time with other men: the singer in another band whose touring schedule crossed the path of our touring schedule about once every two months; and a few nice guys I met on the road. There were dinners, after-hours drinks, bouquets of roses appearing on stage from time to time. It wasn't like I was hopeless—pining away for a married man.

"So," Joey crawled into the van and bounced in his seat. He looked around to make sure we were all there. "Cups full, bladders empty?" This was the signal for go.

"We wanna hear about Troy's week off," Tommy Boy leaned forward and said in a singsong voice. He was the newest member of the band and a few years younger than us. We were breaking him in.

"Zucchini coming ripe?" Joey asked.

"Get a new mulcher?" I said, wanting it to hurt.

"Okay." Troy grabbed the seatbelt and pulled it wide. "If you really must know," he said, pressing the clip hard into the buckle, "she's pregnant."

"Hello," Joey said from behind the wheel.

"When did that happen?" Tommy Boy asked and fell into the back bunk. Since Troy and Susan had gotten married, we'd been traveling nonstop.

"Somewhere between Council Bluffs and Rock Island." Troy rubbed his forehead.

"Damn milkmen," Johnston growled, and I wondered— did the guy ever sleep back there?

♦

On the way out of town, we talked about the usual things—the new Springsteen CD, the new Van Halen video, the confusing part of Led Zeppelin's "Black Dog" where Bonham plays 4/4, and the band plays some other time signature we can never identify, and everything comes back to the one at the chorus.

"Dude, it's a polyrhythm," Joey always said when we asked him to explain it to us. He clearly didn't know the answer either.

We primed each other, trying to recall the name of the manager of the Cat's Paw (Eddie, we thought), and of the bartenders (Rob, the blond one who gave us free shots; and Jim, the one with dark hair, a pitted face, and a mustache, who didn't give us free shots).

And of the waitresses, we could only remember two names—Janice and Jennifer—a pair of long-legged, farm-girl twins with helium voices and matching white-blond hair that ran long and straight as straw down to their waists. It had been four months since we'd played the Cat's Paw, but we remembered the Jensen twins because of how desperately they had wanted Troy, and because of how desperately Joey had wanted them—Joey standing in the stage shadows behind the PA, groaning and grabbing himself as they flipped their hair or bent down to deliver a tray of vodka tonics.

When we reached the western edge of town and passed by Carney's Auto Salvage, the sun reflecting off the ocean of wrecked cars always reminded us that we had reached the three-mile limit. It was a theory of Joey's, based on maritime law. His old man had been in the merchant marine back in the fifties and sixties, before he retired and moved the family to the Midwest, so Joey claimed to know all that could and could not be done on the water.

According to the law of the high seas, Joey said, the three-mile limit to territorial waters decreed that a country's laws only applied within three miles of the coastline. Just outside that point you could fish, gamble, prostitute, and dig for oil, if you wanted, without the intrusion of laws. Each time we left town, we explained to Joey that—legal or illegal—we were unlikely to engage in any of those activities.

"Is that nautical miles," Johnston always wanted to know, "or actual miles?"

"Never mind," Joey would say. "Try to follow along."

Beyond the three-mile limit was a gray zone where regional laws left off and international laws began. Admirality Law gave captains the power to govern their ships.

In our case, Joey explained, that would be him, since he owned the van. And this is why we sometimes called him "Governor" when he became too autocratic about what time we would leave town or what road we should take.

Over time, we'd built on the law, interpreted it broadly, and localized it. Outside the three-mile limit of Carney's wrecking yard on the west side of town, and Big Ed's monster truck speedway on the east, debts were forgotten (who could find us to collect them?), promises to lovers and girlfriends were irrelevant, and wedding vows—forget about it—they dissolved three miles from your wife's doorstep.

Each time we left town, Joey reiterated the theory and added subtle touches and definitions. Today he was stuck on paternity. "This is a tough one," he mumbled behind the wheel. He was stumped. The three-mile limit was supposed to be the ultimate loophole. "But a kid is still your kid, no matter where you go," he said. "I mean, blood follows blood."

Even as Joey said this, I felt the irrevocability of it. Not only was Troy someone's husband now, soon he would be someone's father—cells splitting into more cells—something other than words to bind him. How could this have happened? I had spent more time practicing songs from the seventies with him than Susan had spent on dates with him, more time driving down I-94 with him than Susan had spent married to him.

During a break one night, I remembered my voice getting caught in a tape loop. He'd just yelled to me over the loud music that he and Susan were engaged. I started to yell back, "I want you to be happy." But I got stalled, and all I could say was, "I want, I want, I want." Then something broke through, and I was able to say, "I want you, I want you." Did I ever get to the "be happy" part? I don't think so.

There were times on stage when he seemed so close, nothing more than a thin membrane of noise between us. I waited for that moment in the song, between the chorus and the solo, when he met me center stage and we leaned into each other. Then I'd remind myself to breathe in his sweetness, a mixture of cologne and sweat. After the final song, after the drunks and the last shots, I'd rush back to my motel room, to the bathroom mirror where I'd put my hands to my face, so recently looked at by him. I would search my eyes, study them for what he may have just seen there.

Joey had the radio and heater blasting in the van. The air blew hot in my face. My throat began to burn. It felt raw like something stubborn was stuck there. I hacked and hacked again, trying to cough it out. Troy raised an eyebrow in my direction, as if to say, "I heard that."

In the backseat, Johnston had removed his boots. The sweaty sock odor wafted forward. It wasn't strong, just there—like the smell of something suspicious in the garbage. Tommy Boy lay on a bunk in the back, chain-smoking. The red tip of his cigarette flared each time he took a drag. The sharpness of nicotine entered my brain like a needle threading through my nostrils and sinuses.

I felt the claustrophobia of the moment then, felt the push of the van down the highway. I fought the urge to reach for the key, turn the ignition to deadness. Troy sat in the bucket seat next to me, looking out the window with his chin cradled in two fingers.

Somewhere in the past two years had been intersections, places where his body had been so close to mine that the slight reach of a hand might have resulted in another outcome. I saw all my mistakes then—the times when I should have talked about love instead of guitars, desire instead of amplifiers. The time of all possibilities had passed; I felt it move away like a road sign on the side of the highway.

"So, jerky boy," Johnston said to Troy from the back of the van. "When's the old lady gonna yank your chain?" I had to admit it, Johnston knew how to ask the pointed question. You could almost see it coming. How soon before Troy was one of those longhairs you see in retail stores selling records or stereos or musical equipment?

"Hey, man," Troy raised his hands and yelled over the music. "I don't even want to think about it."

✦

After a total of two gas breaks and three pee stops in nine hours, we neared Billings just as the day was starting to lose its light. It was a few hours before we'd reach the foothills and begin to move through the passes and feel the rush of elevations changing. The mountain ranges would be in darkness by then, but we had seen the scaly rock faces in the distance enough times—gauged the progress of our movement by their peaks—that we would feel them like a silent presence around us.

Driving through Billings, we passed by a gray refinery with a complicated web of ladders and dusty pipes going on for miles. In the distance was a high row of towers with flashing lights sparking at the top through plumes of smoke. On the west edge of town, the refineries turned to car dealerships and then to housing developments that thinned into tilled farmland.

We were running low on gas. "E-minor" is what Joey called this, yelling it out like a chord change in a jam session, so we'd begin to look for exits. We avoided the quick stops—inconvenience stores, we called them—with slightly lewd names like Kum & Go, or Pump & Party. If we were low on jerky and desperate, we might pull into a Holiday or Casey's.

We took the Laurel exit west of Billings, coming to rest in front of a graying wood structure that was built to look like an old-style trading post. The hand-painted sign on the front said, Red's Thirsty Mule, in dripping crimson letters. Joey pulled the van up next to a faded green gas pump. The glass cover had been punched in and the per gallon price changed to 19 cents.

Joey ground out his cigarette in the ashtray and cracked the driver's side door. It fell open with a loud clank. The rest of us rolled out of the right side, stretched our legs, rolled our necks. We were empty but not hungry, tired but not ready to sleep.

The facade of Red's had log cabin walls made of rough timbers and a sagging roof of wooden slats for shingles. Out front was a mock swinging door and an old-fashioned wild-west sidewalk with a hitching-post bike rack that looked like you could tie horse reins to it.

On a bear-and-eagle totem pole to the right, a column of placards listed a few of Red's attractions—Gas, Showers, Bait & Tackle, Outfitting, Spirits, Drive-Thru Espresso, Indian Art, Off-Sale. Inside to the right, the cashier sat behind the counter surrounded by Navaho blankets, raccoon hats, velvet paintings, and silver and turquoise jewelry. On shelves around the small store were the usual products like Alka-Seltzer and Coke, Doritos and Quaker State motor oil.

"Bathrooms to the left." Johnston turned, and we all moved down the narrow hallway. There was a bar on the right, fenced in by a half-wall and a row of tables. I looked inside as I walked. Happy hour had started. A few men in denim work shirts and a few women with big hair sat at the bar. A jukebox played a country song. There was a Budweiser sign on the far wall, the crack of pool balls.

I joined a line outside the bathroom. The woman in front of me was holding an infant and trying to rein in a talky toddler. The little girl wanted to touch everything. She cranked the lever of the stuffed animal claw machine. She rattled the coin return slot of the low pay phones with her sticky fingers, then begged her mother for a quarter.

"Honey, no," the woman kept saying, "no, no, no." She shifted the baby to her right hip, brought the quilted diaper bag full of lotions and baby bottles onto her shoulder, and jerked the toddler into place with her left hand.

Troy came out of the men's bathroom, raised his eyebrows at the crowd of women in the hallway. Tommy Boy went into the men's. I stepped forward and jiggled the locked knob of the women's.

"It's in use," the young mother said.

"Just a second," a wobbly voice echoed inside.

Directly behind me were two dishwater blonds wearing too much patchouli for close spaces. The smell was strong and musky as fur on the tongue. They looked about twenty. They both had their hair bound in small, messy braids that ran clear up to the scalp like some white girl version of dreadlocks.

They wore skintight tank tops, as if they were trying to press summer into October. They stood in the hallway, their thin shoulders hunched and shivering in the cold. They didn't speak, just giggled and munched down long coils of string licorice. The girl on the right had a black bra peeking out from under the narrow straps of her tank top; the girl on the left was wearing red.

Tommy Boy came out of the men's, smiled at the two blonds, and pushed his own long blond bangs away from his face. The two girls looked at Tommy Boy, then dove for the open door of the men's.

Just then the women's cracked open and two older ladies appeared in the doorway. One moved slowly with the help of a metal walker that clanked down hard in front of her every step.

"So sorry," said the lady with the wobbly voice, who supported her friend with the walker by the elbow. We cleared a space for them to get through, and the young mother gathered up her children and her diaper bag and disappeared into the women's.

I took the next bathroom that opened up—the men's—when the dreadlocks were done flushing and laughing. The water felt cool on my face. I put in some eyedrops, slapped on a little makeup and some lipstick, ran a brush through my hair.

It only took a few minutes. By the time I came down the narrow hallway, I heard the low rumble of Troy's laughter in the bar. The blonds were huddled next to him, their thin bottoms propped up against a pool table. Johnston was chalking up a cue, and Tommy Boy was leaning at the bar with a ten-dollar bill in his hand.

"So you guys are in a band," I heard the one with the black bra say as I passed by. A little thrill ran through her voice. "Cool." And then they both started giggling.

Joey was waiting in the van. "Where are those guys?" he asked.

"This might take a while," I said, ripping open a package of jerky. Mostly I loved the saltiness, loved the way my mouth watered at the first bite. I liked how hard my teeth had to work to tear off the smallest chunk. At the bottom of every package of jerky was a feeling of accomplishment, a kind of Mount Everest moment.

I wasn't even finished with the first strip when Tommy

Boy burst through the front door of Red's. He ran to the van with a big smile on his face and rapped on Joey's window.

"Go ahead without us," he said, trying to catch his breath. "We'll catch up to you guys later."

"Ah, no," Joey said, rubbing his eyes hard. "I don't think so." It was easy to imagine Joey and me tomorrow, unloading equipment and setting up without them. How many songs could a drummer and a singer do alone?

"Are they sisters?" I asked, my voice sounding low and gruff, strange even to my ears.

"Naw," Tommy Boy answered, "cousins." He shuffled his feet in the cold parking lot.

"They said they'd drive us to Bozeman," he explained, motioning west with his thumb. He shook his thick bangs out of his eyes, and looked to me for support. At that moment, his face appeared angelic in the half darkness.

"C'mon, *Gov*," I said. Who were we to stand in the way of initiation?

"Oh, hell," Joey said finally, then poked the kid in the chest. "You get a half hour." He shoved the van into first and released the parking brake. "After that, we're leaving."

We rolled into a parking spot in front of Red's. Tommy Boy hooted and ran past us, slapping the hood of the van.

"You're only young once," Joey said, mostly to himself. He turned the ignition to auxiliary, adjusted the radio, put his boots up on the dash, and noodled his toothpick in his mouth. He seemed old and fusty to me then, like he was wearing an unraveling cardigan and handing out the keys to the Buick on a Saturday night.

✦

After a few minutes of waiting, Joey joined the other guys in Red's. I crawled in the back of the van and stretched out on the couch. I pulled my long coat tight under my chin and tried to sleep. The day had gone on too long, and my voice had gone hoarse too quickly. I lay in the darkness, my throat burning raw with every pulse.

Lately I'd been feeling like my life was a movie in serious need of editing. I wanted one of those fast-forward sections, like in *Rocky* when you see Stallone roll out of bed, suck down a raw egg concoction, and stagger out the door for a predawn run. The back of his gray sweatpants barely disappear down the car-lined street when the scene flashes to him doing one-handed push-ups in the gym.

Next we see him in a meat locker throwing his bloody fists into hanging carcasses like punching bags. Then he's huffing up the steps of Independence Hall—a deep V of sweat spreading down his neckline. The theme song builds when he jogs up the many steps, which look precarious as a scaling wall thanks to the camera angle.

When he reaches the top, his arms shoot up in victory and the chorus swells—*Gonna fly now*—the camera rising and swallowing him in a panoramic view. In five minutes, Rocky goes from fat slug to fighting dynamo, because all we really want is to see him pummel the genetically superior Russian.

In that moment alone in the van, I wanted to take a scalpel to the last two years of my life, wanted to watch the unimportant days and weeks fall into curls at my feet. I wanted to keep the good parts, splice them together without interruption, arrange them so that they added up differently.

I must have fallen asleep quickly. It seemed like no time passed before Joey and Johnston came back to the van, bringing with them the gritty smell of cigarettes. Johnston piled in the front seat, and Joey started up the van, the cold air giving way to the warm.

"Crazy bitches," Johnston said under his breath, pulling the bag out of the glove compartment. He cupped a Zig-Zag between his fingers and sprinkled in some pot. He licked the long edge of the paper, then twisted it up in one smooth motion.

"Nipple rings *and* tongue studs." Johnston shuddered. *"Ouch."* He brought the joint to his lips, smoothed out the edges with his tongue.

"Did they show you, too?" Joey said, incredulous.

"I asked nicely," Johnston answered and lit up the tip, the cherry flaming red in the darkness.

"Damn Montana girls," Joey said, taking the joint. He sucked deep, hiccuped, then sucked deep again. "They'll rope you and tie you for sure." He let out his words in one slow wheeze.

I sat up and pushed my coat aside. Joey passed the joint back to me, and I took a hit. The smoke felt strangely smooth on my throat, rolling in as easily as fog.

"What time is it?" I asked.

"Time to go," Joey said.

"I'll get them," I said, pulling on my coat. "I gotta pee anyway." I slid open the side door and stepped out. It didn't look that late—not deep dark, just dark—maybe around eight o'clock.

I went inside Red's, waved at the cashier behind the counter, who now seemed to know all of us, and turned left for the bathrooms. Passing the bar, I saw Tommy Boy sitting at a table with the dreadlocked blond in the red bra. She must have been talking calculus, because one of Tommy Boy's hands was bent possessively over the neck of his Bud and the other was propping up the side of his head. The other blond was nowhere in sight and neither was Troy.

I went to the bathroom, washed my hands, cranked the paper towels out of the dispenser one by one. I took my time reading the graffiti, which told me that this place was hell and it was hopeless—I would never escape. The messages also cautioned me to stay away from Doug and urged me to try lesbian sex.

I heard the noises in the other bathroom. It was impossible not to hear them—some laughing and talking, some scuffling of feet, the bump and brush of bodies against the common wall. What was I supposed to do about that? I opened the door and headed down the hallway, running into the blond from the bar on my way out. She must have been coming to retrieve her friend. She smiled at me, like she knew I was just the chick in the band and I wasn't going to beat her up.

Tommy Boy was in the van by the time I got back. Johnston was in the backseat stretched out on the bunk.

"I *would* get the one who was pre-med," Tommy Boy said. He'd been with us for three months. So far, his innocence was the only thing with staying power.

Just then Troy came through the front door of Red's with the two blond dreadlocks tucked on either side of him. They waved good-bye to us, and we waved good-bye to them.

"You got a nose for brainy women." Johnston said. "Live with it."

Troy stood on the wild-west sidewalk for a few minutes with the blonde in the black bra. She leaned into him, slung her arms around his waist, and rested her right cheek on his chest. He reached around his back and returned her hands to her side.

"At least your genes will do well," I said.

Tommy Boy moaned in the back seat. "But I wanted my jeans to do well."

"There's always the Cat's Paw," Joey said, laying on the horn. Troy looked up then, as if he'd been waiting for the sound.

"And the Rusty Nail and the Zoo and the Golden Spike," Johnston added in a monotone, listing the next three clubs we were playing. If you couldn't get lucky in those places, you just plain weren't lucky.

On the sidewalk, Troy turned to the blond and mouthed something like "Gotta go." She looked up at him with a sly smile, said something like "See ya later" and walked to her car. Troy turned for the van, pulling his collar high around his neck.

As soon as he reached the van, Troy opened the door and said, "Nothing happened," in a voice full of impatience, like it was a press conference and he would not be taking questions. He slid into the front bucket and slammed the door hard. Johnston groaned in the backseat.

"Okay," Joey said and raised his eyebrows. "If you say so."

"Really," Troy looked around. He swept his hands out in one clean motion. "Nothing."

Joey put the van in reverse, backed out of the spot and headed for the frontage road. "She pre-med, too?" Joey finally asked.

"Nah." Troy rubbed his hands together, blowing warmth into them. "She wants to play guitar," he said, his voice sounding tired.

We all started to laugh. Girls who wanted to play guitar—the countryside was full of them. "Do you know barre chords?" Johnston whispered in a falsetto in the backseat. Tommy Boy fell into the bunk, grabbed his stomach, and laughed miserably.

"She has her dad's old Strat from the sixties," Troy said. "Sunburst finish."

"A sixty-two?" I guessed. From hanging around these guys, I could almost write the manual on Fenders.

"Nah," Troy answered, "she thinks he got it around fifty-seven."

Johnston whistled low. We all knew what that probably meant—a solid maple neck.

"It's got some belt buckle dings on the back," Troy said.

"A little mileage," said Joey, pulling the van onto the freeway. "You can't fault a guitar for that."

Tommy Boy leaned forward with renewed interest. "Original pickups?" he asked.

"Been in the attic since Woodstock." Troy looked forward into the dark windshield.

"Oh, man," Tommy Boy said, lust in his voice. "I bet she's dripping with tone."

Joey pressed down on the accelerator and shifted through the gears, the headlights clearing a path through the darkness. Everyone was quiet for a long time thinking about the waste—a cherry Strat lying unplayed in its tweed case under some girl-who-wants-to-play-guitar's bed.

"She gonna bring it out to the club?" Tommy Boy finally asked.

"Maybe Thursday." Troy started to chuckle then as if surprised by his own luck.

"My man," Joey said, slugging Troy on the shoulder like he'd just returned from some long journey. And I knew he was right. All talk of bed linens and window blinds was now a thing of the past. Then I thought about Susan back home in Pleasant Hills. Even as we spoke, she was probably shopping for cribs and car seats. The three-mile limit said that whatever happened out here didn't follow us home—and that was a code. But I still wondered about those sounds in the bathroom. I wondered about them for myself.

"So it was all business with you and the dreadlock?" I asked, trying to sound like another nosy guy in the band. "The two of you, just shooting the breeze about licks and riffs?"

"Pretty much," Troy said, looking me square in the face.

"And she didn't even want your body," I pressed.

He shifted around in the bucket seat. He flipped open the glove compartment and reached inside for the bag of pot. He exhaled deep.

"I told her to think hard about me at midnight," he said, unrolling the plastic bag down to the bottom.

He pinched his fingers into the green and stared straight ahead, as if talking to the dashboard. "And I told her I would be thinking hard about her at the same time." His voice fell flat as he said this.

"At the stroke of midnight?" Joey asked.

"Kinda like that." Troy sniffed and popped a crease into the Zig-Zag.

"Sex by proxy," Johnston said from the backseat, and everyone started to laugh.

"Aw, jerky boy." Joey pounded the wheel. "The ultimate loophole."

It was hard to think of anything to say after that. We rode for a long time in silence. Troy finished rolling the joint and passed it to me, holding the lighter as I fired it up. I passed the joint back to him and he smiled at me, a hangdog grin of perfect white teeth.

"C'mon, Ninj," he said, as if it mattered to ask forgiveness of the wrong woman.

Even before he met Susan, I had imagined him walking down church steps, wearing an immaculate tuxedo. He was surrounded by friends, bells chiming in the background, that same grin brilliant against the crispness of his collar.

That night in the van, he looked brushed-down and smooth as velvet to me, like so many hands had invested all time and care in him. I knew he would always be some woman's treasure. I fought my own hand's impulse to reach up and touch his face.

Outside, the inky blackness swallowed us. Aside from headlights and moonlight, we were flying blind. Clusters of light from small towns appeared in the distance from time to time. They floated on the glassy surface of the horizon like tiny buoys. They came closer, then disappeared as we passed them in the night.

DYLAN'S LOST YEARS

Somewhere between Hibbing and New York, the red rust streets of the Iron Range and the shipping yards of the Atlantic, somewhere between Zimmerman and Dylan was a pit stop in Fargo, a Superman-in-the-phone-booth interlude, recalled by no one but the Danforth brothers, who hired the young musician, fresh in town with his beat-up six-string and his small-town twang, to play shake, rattle, and roll, to play good golly, along with Wayne on the keys and Dirk on the bass, two musical brothers whom you might still find playing the baby grand, happy hours at the southside Holiday Inn.

And if you slip the snifter a five, Wayne might talk between how high the moon, and embraceable you, about Dylan's lost years, about the Elvis sneer, the James Dean leather collar pulled tight around his neck, about the late-night motorcycle rides, kicking over the city's garbage cans, and how they finally had to let him go, seeing how he was more trouble than he was worth, and with everyone in full agreement that the new boy just could not sing.

THE MOVIE OF THE WORLD

They fired their drummer, Bobby Loud, quite suddenly that afternoon when they went to pick him up and he informed them through the locked apartment door that he wasn't coming.

"I'm sick," he yelled from behind the peephole. Their drummer's full name was Robert Frank, or R. F. Loud, which he liked to tell people stood for real fucking loud, but mostly they called him Bobby. The band stood outside his apartment, taking turns pounding with their bare fists. The brass knocker clanked on its metal plate. The cardboard-thin door rattled in its frame.

Lately they'd been missing gigs for reasons out of their control—a tornado in Grand Island, a blown gasket in Kenosha, a gone-bad girlfriend who slashed all their tires in Des Moines. Acts of god, forces of nature, they thought. But they worked for an agency that didn't believe in sickness or malady of any kind. *The only reason for missing a gig is death,* their booking agent often said, *and only your own.*

When they got the last-minute call for a one-nighter, to fill in for some other unlucky band stuck in Omaha with a cracked engine block, they knew this was a chance to make it up to the agency. Their drummer might have understood all this if he ever talked to their booking agent, but Bobby Loud spoke only to his girlfriend, Bunny, who was now giggling with him on the other side of the door.

"I've been throwing up all day," their drummer moaned. His voice was muffled and weak-sounding. Too weak, they thought—suspiciously weak. They listened closer. Someone said he heard a bag of potato chips crinkling.

"We'll have to cancel," Bobby Loud said, his voice growing fainter as he seemed to move away from the door.

The band stood in the hallway and listened hard. Someone thought he heard the rolling churn of bathwater in the background; someone swore he heard a champagne bottle uncorking.

Outside it was a hot summer afternoon. It would be sweltering inside the bus where all the girlfriends waited. The bus was a converted red-and-black seventy-four-passenger with devil's horns and a skull and crossbones painted on the hood, and their name, Bad Reputation, sprawled in anarchy-red letters on the side. The bus was gassed up, loaded with equipment, and double-parked on Clark Street with its flashers going.

The basement hallway of Bobby Loud's building was cool and dark. The band hated to go out into the sweltering day. They leaned their backs against the wall, rattled the doorknob, smoked, and tried to wait their drummer out. In the other apartments, children wailed and vacuum cleaners howled. All the yelling for Bobby Loud and the pounding of their fists shook the building. Up and down the hallway they heard safety chains sliding into metal guides.

All of Bad Reputation was present—their guitarists, Vinny One and Vinny Two, twin brothers known more for their waist-length manes of dark curly hair and their matching roman noses than for their guitar playing, which was nervous and cluttered and included lots of leaping around at the end of songs. Their younger brother, Vinny Three, was also present. He was the bass player in the band and looked like a smaller, younger, shorter-haired version of his older brothers.

At one time they'd had their own band, also called the Vinnys, until their youngest brother, Vinny Four—who did not resemble his brothers at all, who had arctic blue eyes and long blond hair that fell in lapping swirls on his shoulders like wedding cake icing—had decided to go to college and become a chemical engineer. That was when the remaining three Vinnys branched out and merged with the members of Bad Reputation.

Their lead singer, Blaze, was with them in Bobby Loud's apartment building. She was new to the band, and still an unknown to them. She was forever humming, they noticed, and looking down empty hallways. She was tall with the delicate face of a waif and translucent skin that seemed to emit a faint light. Her hair was long and curly and dyed an impossible shade of primary red that roared like the flag of a third world country against her white skin and her all-black clothes.

Bad Reputation's road crew also waited in the hallway with the band. The lighting team, Hodgie and Duke, hung back from the door, sticking close enough to support their soundman, Gunner, who led the effort to coax Bobby Loud out of the apartment.

Gunner was big, with beefy forearms like jack hammers and a long, blond shag haircut that made him look more like an all-star wrestler than a soundman. "Honey." Gunner brought his voice down to a reasonable whisper. It was time to speak directly to Bobby Loud's girlfriend, bypassing their drummer, because they were all now convinced that she had their drummer bound up in some mother-witch-sex-hex. Gunner leaned in and pressed his wide forehead to the door, trying to look backward into the peephole.

"C'mon, Honey," he called through the door as if he were someone's drunk and locked-out husband.

Gunner had nicknames for everyone. People were *peeps;* fans were *bangers;* rude fans were *z-bangers;* people who smoked were *ciggie kings.* He called their new singer Blaze because of her flaming red hair, and he called Bunny, their drummer's girlfriend, Honey, because that's what Bobby Loud called her *(Honey, can you hand me my smokes? Honey, can you rub my neck?).* But is wasn't just Honey. It was *Honey,* in a high, wobbly, hundred-year-old woman's voice.

"C'mon, Honey," Gunner and Hodgie and Duke took turns calling through the door. "Can Bobby come out and play?" But there was no response. No sound of reluctant breathing or second thoughts on the other side—just the light sounds of splashing water and laughter in the distance.

After a while, after Honey did not appear and Bobby did not appear, and the sucking sounds of bathwater draining had ceased, the band trudged single file down the hallway.

On the way out, Gunner stopped by the front door and threw an elbow into their former drummer's mailbox, crumpling in the small bin by aiming directly for the hand-lettered sign that said, B. LOUD, in all caps.

Gunner had not always been a soundman. Sometime earlier in his life he had dreams of being a drummer. He even bought one of those four-piece Buddy Rich starter kits in high school. It was beautiful—pearl white, with a snare, a kick, a tom-tom, a hi-hat, and a fifteen-inch crash cymbal that rang hollow as a bad punch line when you hit it.

Sometimes after school he would sit for hours in the band room practicing his triplets, his fills, his rolls, until the band teacher sat down in the semicircle of the practice room one day and said, "Just add water, kid," meaning, Gunner assumed, that without some missing ingredient his playing was dry and square as a box cake. But that was years ago, and now he was their soundman.

In the back of the bus, he and Blaze sat on the high bunk. They kicked their legs and rocked side to side as the red-and-black bus roared down the highway.

"Damn," Gunner whispered. He turned to Blaze. "If only I hadn't bragged up my jazz band days so much."

"It's okay," she said and put her hand on his shoulder. She knew all about going too far. "Sometimes on those late-night drives, you get talking," she whispered, "and memory just blooms like a rose."

Outside the long row of bus windows, the flat landscape rolled by like frames from a movie—pasture, pasture, hill, pasture, telephone pole, pasture—as the bus bumped down the road. Maybe at one time kids with braces and long braids popped their gum and rode in straight lines in this bus, but now the seats had been ripped from their safety bolts and replaced with a circle of tattered couches—dull browns and greens, castoffs from the sixties, bought for five bucks apiece at St. Vincent de Paul.

The whole band of Vinnys sat on the couches reading magazines about guitar playing. Beside them, their tall cool-blond girlfriends sprawled out and read magazines about fashion. But no one was really reading. Behind the glossy pages, everyone had their eyes on Gunner as he perched overhead in the high bunk.

"Before they make the movie of the world," Blaze said, looking at Gunner to make sure she had his attention, "they should cut out all the cars and telephone poles and people, and make one long shot of the horizon." She pointed outside, stretching her thin arm to show the panoramic view. She'd been on the road too long and with too many bands. She referred to the world outside in not-quite-real terms. Since she was new to this band, no one had disagreed with her yet.

"Yes," Gunner said, trying to keep the conversation going. "Very dramatic," he added when the bus became too silent. "Outside these windows runs the unending movie of the world."

Bad Reputation cruised north on Highway 75, every minute and every mile bringing them closer to this drummerless night. Behind their backs was a bearing wall their road crew had constructed to keep the equipment in its own half of the bus. They felt the shift and groan of black boxes and power amps and cords whenever they made a turn. And it was this heavy shifting that reminded them of the absence of Bobby Loud.

They knew they had Bobby Loud's black orchid, twenty-piece Tama drum set loaded in the back of the bus, complete with double bass drums, two snares, and an acreage of floor toms, mounted toms, and spinning roto-toms on top.

They knew they had Bobby Loud's tuned cowbells. He was famous for setting them up in the farthest corner of the stage away from his kit, then walking to them on his hands during the middle of drum solos. Everyone would wait quietly as he beat out the notes for "Chopsticks" or "Three Blind Mice" with two drumsticks duct taped to a special pair of shoes, then he'd walk on his hands back to his drums and finish his solo. The crowd would go wild. How were they ever going to replace him?

They knew they had Bobby Loud's Paiste cymbals and his twenty-inch Zildjian medium ride and his bongos and his special padded drum throne. They had everything but Bobby Loud himself. And this is why all eyes were on their soundman perched in the high bunk, who could fake a backbeat if pressed.

"Damn," Gunner shuddered again, feeling the weight of Bobby Loud's drum set lurching behind the bearing wall. Blaze felt it too. She threw her body back on the bunk and let out a high, pained laugh. All the cool-blond girlfriends looked up from the fashion magazines they were pretending to read. In the darkness of the high bunk, Blaze's glossy skin and pale green eyes made her red hair burn even more acutely.

"What," Gunner looked at them and said. He leaned back

and messed up the singer's hair. "What?" he said to her.

It was just past Halstad, when they declared a police state and voted unanimously to promote Gunner to the job of drummer. Drastic times, drastic measures.

"Ah, c'mon, guys," Gunner moaned. As a roadie he was an employee and had no vote. After he was promoted to drummer he acquired a vote, but by then it was too late—the vote had been cast.

Just as quickly they promoted Hodgie, their lightman and driver, to the job of soundman. They appointed Duke their spotman to run the lights, and they asked Rita, Duke's girlfriend, who was just along for the ride, to run the spot for the night.

They did all this within sixty miles, also nicknaming Rita *Pleats* because she was wearing baggy, pleated khakis, and they knew Gunner had enough to worry about without having to come up with nicknames.

Even as their bus cruised down the highway, Bad Reputation knew they did not look as bad-ass as they would have liked, and that something was bound to go wrong. About ten miles from the club, the bus began to sputter. It coughed and lunged down the highway, angling for the emergency lane.

"You bitch," Hodgie said from behind the wheel. Anything that failed him was automatically female. The engine clunked and the bus slowed to a halt, the sound of gravel crackling under their tires. Hodgie pounded the wide steering wheel and looked back at the rest of the band.

"Try the key," one of the Vinnys said. The ignition was touchy, as were the tires, the transmission, and the brakes.

It was a touchy bus, a bus that required coaxing.

"Did you try the choke?" someone offered. Someone must always say this.

"Yes, goddammit," Hodgie said, trying the ignition. The engine whirred lower and lower. "Shit," he said, pounding the steering wheel. "Shit, shit, shit."

At the sound of the dead engine, Blaze rolled from the top bunk in a tangle of blankets and hair. She landed on her feet and pulled on her coat, heading for the door. She grabbed the silver pole and swung her body around, landing on the bottom step just in time for Hodgie to swing open the doors.

When they hired her to be their lead singer, they had no idea she might bring other talents to the band, the best of which was her natural gift for soliciting roadway assistance. Something about the sight of her with jumper cables made a man go for his brakes. And whenever they found themselves in the middle of the night out of gas in some small town in the middle of nowhere, her voice like honey-over-gravel always persuaded the local cop to come and open the gas station.

"I'm just passing through, and I seem to have run low on gas," she'd drawl into the pay phone in her most helpless Southern accent. And after she hung up the receiver, a cop would appear, following the vapor trail to the dark gas station where he'd expect to find one stranded woman with gorgeous pipes, but instead was greeted by a pack of scraggly musicians wanting to buy gas, wanting change for the pop machine.

She felt some of her best work was done on the highway. "Get down!" she yelled at everybody in the bus and walked around to the side of the road. One look at those guys, she knew, and no one would stop.

This time it worked like it always worked. Before her rescuer saw the whole band—those flat mugs that looked vaguely like some crazy guy you'd seen at 4 A.M. lurking behind the vanilla cremes in the 7-11—it was too late. The hood was thrown open, the ground post hooked up to the bus battery, and all that precious juice was flowing from one engine to another.

Hodgie spun the engine. A cheer went up in the bus.

"Thanks a lot, man," she said and dropped the hood, leaving the man holding the cables as the bus revved onto the road, the gallery of faces inside waving at him, signaling thumbs-up through the long row of windows. She jumped on, and they passed by, heading north on Highway 75.

The Level Seven was an asymmetrical wonderland with winding staircases leading to crooked balconies. Until recently, it had been a disco. Blaze descended the steps to the dressing room, navigating the shaky stairs in her stilettos. The incline was steep. There were no handrails, yet she flew down them loose-limbed, never once thinking of falling.

So far it had been a long drummerless night. They had arrived on time and loaded their gear in the back door. They'd had no trouble setting up Bobby Loud's drums. Gunner often set up the kit when their drummer disappeared to the bathroom or the back room of the club. Bobby Loud had mysterious friends and mysterious things to do in every city they played.

They'd made it through the sound check and the warm-up. The first two sets had been mild, functional disasters—miscues, play-throughs, muffed fills—but nothing truly bad had happened. At least they hadn't had to stop in the middle of a song and talk about it. It was nearly midnight, and they had one more set to go. Twelve songs, tops. If they stretched solos, they were home free.

The only good thing about discos, Blaze thought, was that they made decent rock clubs when the mirror ball stopped spinning. As she walked down the stairs, she counted the club's levels. There were supposed to be seven, but she could only count six: the two balconies (one stage right and high, one stage left and medium-high); and there were two kidney bean–shaped raised platforms behind the bar. That made four levels.

To the bottom right and left of the stage were two lower-level caverns, which the band called the snakepits. These were the waitressless and bouncerless regions where there was a pipe in every pocket and a pint in every purse. From the snakepits, the audience could only view small slices of the band, so they lost interest quickly.

It wasn't unusual for some guy from the pits to yell "take it off," or "show us your tits," or for some woman with a hoarse voice to scream "take a break" during the quiet moments between songs. The band had figured out a way to deal with the snakepits. They aimed two PA columns directly into the caverns. That way, if things got ugly, they could fumigate with sheer volume.

In the basement of the Level Seven, Blaze made her way to the dressing room. She walked by the discarded boxes, the empty kegs stacked against the wall, and the sullen bartender on break sitting at a card table smoking a cigarette.

She moved past the dusty deep freeze where all the frozen pizzas were stored and passed through the stale smoke and the yeasty smell of spilled beer, finally coming to their dressing room—a small windowless space filled with four walls of graffiti and all the broken tables and three-legged chairs from upstairs.

The rest of the band was in the dressing room, running through scales on their guitars, smoking, and sitting on old couches with their feet propped up on broken chairs.

A woeful history was recorded on the dressing room walls of the Level Seven. It was like an archaeological find. There were stenciled peace signs left over from the sixties and enthusiastic boasts from now-unknown bands from the seventies—*Titanica Rules, Yeah!*

There were diatribes against booking agents that could have been written yesterday (*Johnny Youngblood is a Nazi*), and there was much general whining (*Pamela, call the doctor. I'm not feeling so well*). Blaze read the wall, thinking of all the stranded musicians who had passed through this room, recording their complaints on the once smooth sheet of concrete.

"You gotta think groove," Vinny One was lecturing Gunner, who sat on the couch nodding and clicking Bobby Loud's drumsticks on a pockmarked trunk that rested in between the couches like a coffee table.

"Forget this *tic, tic, tic*," Vinny Two said to Gunner. He bent over in his chair, sucked deep on a burned-out roach, and passed it to Vinny One. Gunner nodded. He held the drum sticks in a loose jazz grip. By nature Gunner was a meticulous person.

They had all observed how, as a soundman, he seemed pleased by the way the knobs on his soundboard sat in neat, polished rows. They'd noticed that he was always aware of the location of the roll of duct tape and sometimes hoarded it, because it was common knowledge in any band that whoever controlled the roll of duct tape wielded enormous power.

He never touched a drop of alcohol while running sound, and he'd told several band members in confidence that a bowel movement between sets could take him out of the mixing zone and ruin the rest of the night.

Already, in his first night as a drummer, he had confessed fears that breaking the order of any of his carefully constructed rituals would anger the gods of rhythm and cause him to miss fills and play through breaks.

"Forget control," Vinny One said, and pushed back his long curly hair. "Think loud." Working together, the Vinnys were trying to teach Gunner the Vinny family philosophy of noise. It was the only way Bad Reputation knew how to break through to the groove.

"I'm no Loud," Gunner confessed.

Thank God, Blaze thought. Bobby Loud played long drum rolls across his eight-piece roto-tom spread. He rambled over the beat, came out long, came out short, forced the band to adjust to him when he came back to the snare for the two and the four. Bobby Loud was a study in noise, hulking over his drum set, holding his sticks like they were ham hocks.

"Nobody wants you to be the Loud," all three Vinnys roared in unison.

"God, no," Blaze agreed. She was in the corner of the dressing room changing clothes behind a wet bar. She bent low as she slipped into her next outfit. With each new set and each new outfit, she revealed more and more of herself. Each gig was like a game of strip poker. Now, in the last set, she was down to a leather body suit that looked like it had been buffed onto her skin.

"Hey, guys," she called out from under the bar, "where do you think the seventh level is?" No one answered. They had all climbed the stairs back to the stage to get tuned and ready for the last set. Blaze plopped down on a couch and put up her tired feet. Her four-inch heels rubbed hard against the ball of her foot. What kind of sadist dreamed up these shoes, she thought, and what kind of masochist wears them?

She lit one of the Vinnys' perfectly rolled joints and scanned the dressing room walls, reading them like a newspaper for messages from anyone she knew. The best thing she found was a sketch about their booking agency, the Great Music Organization, otherwise known as GMO, but most often referred to by musicians as the Great Mileage Organization due to their slingshot method of routing bands.

The sketch was a map of the continental United States, very well drawn, with the rings of a dart board superimposed over it. In the sketch, a blindfolded booking agent with a heavy black mustache threw wild darts at the board— now Topeka, now Denver, now Pittsburgh, now Omaha. Underneath the caption read, *GMO booking practices.*

"The stage," she said out loud, although no one was there to hear it. "The stage is level seven!" She was a little stunned then, to think of all the times she had hung over the edge of the stage, never once understanding where she might be singing from.

It was a regular weeknight—slow, small clusters of people sitting around tables, nursing their drinks. The day workers had gone home to bed; the partiers to better parties. All that was left were the drinkers with nowhere better to go, and they seemed to be enjoying the taped break music more than the band's live sets. They jumped up to dance when the break music came on and even applauded after each song.

This was residual from the disco days. Like the lighted hopscotch dance floor and the rotating mirror ball, disco was a stubborn ghost that haunted the club. As soon as the band started playing, the dancers would leave the floor, grab up their sequined jackets, and move to tables at the far end of the bar. They still wanted to lean in and say sexy disco-day things to each other, but Bad Reputation played too loud for conversation.

On break, Gunner was out in the crowd, drinking Coke with ice in a frosty glass. He mingled and tried to control his nerves, leaving his drink resting on the bar as he turned to talk to people in the aisles. He moved, and he laughed. He flirted with anyone who flirted with him. Just past midnight—one more set to go.

Soon he climbed on stage for the third set and went through his ritual. In one short evening of playing drums, he had already established a routine. First, he wiped his forehead on a clean white hand towel that he kept on a hook beside the floor tom, then he wiped his hands on the towel and hung it back on the hook. He rubbed his hands on his thighs once for luck, and he flicked his hair back in a quick motion with both hands. After that, he picked up his drumsticks, one at a time—left one first, then the right.

Although it was dark on stage, everyone in the band knew this routine because they'd watched him go through the motions before every song they'd performed that evening. Gunner's towel ritual increased the down time between songs to about two minutes.

"Gunner, remember, try to go from one song to the next," Vinny One leaned backed and yelled. "No down time."

"Okay," Gunner said, picking up his sticks. They felt too thick. "Something's not right," he said, but no one heard.

The lights were turned low. Everybody waited in the dark for the four-count to start the first song. Gunner picked up a flashlight. He checked the size of the sticks and found they were right. As the lights came up, Blaze noticed an alarmed look on Gunner's face. He was perked up like a dog who had heard a tone too high for anyone else's ears.

He clicked the sticks four times, and they lumbered off following the plodding beat like it was a road rushing out before them, because the beat was the only way Bad Reputation knew how to get where they wanted to go. They followed him up hills, around curves, and through the mountains, until about five minutes later he returned them to the place where they started.

The echo of the last chord fell like a heavy velvet curtain. The lights went down. There was a smattering of applause, more talking. Blaze looked back at Gunner. He was concentrating very hard now on his fingernails. He had his flashlight again, and he was biting and inspecting, biting and inspecting. He stood up, reached into his pocket for a nail clipper. Then he sat and began to clip away at his nails.

Blaze climbed through the first layer of cords, slipped through a space between amps. "Gunner," she hissed, "the song. Get to the song." He was busy now working on his cuticles.

"All right, all right." He waved his hand at her, picking up his sticks. He studied their length. Hmm, funny.

"Thick?" she asked.

"Yeah," he grinned. "Strangest thing."

He checked the size again with the flashlight, took his time with his white hand towel, then they were off. All three Vinnys were looking at Blaze for clues. All around she saw brows knitted over roman noses, cocked curly-haired heads.

After the next song was over, Gunner swerved around on his seat and stared up at the neon backdrop. He gazed at the sign for several minutes with his back to the band.

Blaze climbed through equipment again to get behind the drum set where Gunner sat cushioned between the wall and the kit. It was cozy back there behind Bobby Loud's drum set, like being strapped tight in a sports car—all gadgets ready, something for every appendage to do.

"You can see the gas move through the tubes," he told her when she pulled up next to him. "But you have to look really close." Gunner and Blaze turned around and watched the neon for a while.

"Hey," they heard a Vinny behind them. "Today or tomorrow?"

Gunner and Blaze stared at each other, then stared back through the layers of cymbals and tom-toms at the rest of the band. All the Vinnys stared back at them like a triple hallucination, hands poised on the necks of their guitars.

"I can't," Gunner barely whispered.

"Sure you can," Blaze said. "You're doing it."

"No," Gunner put up a hand. It wobbled slightly. "Something's wrong." His sticks were still in his hands. Blaze looked around and noticed that the towel was still untouched on its little hook. Something *was* wrong. She asked Duke to bring up the drum lights, tilted Gunner's head back and looked into his eyes. His pupils were wide and dark, spreading into ovals of black. There was no trace of Gunner's ragged blue eyes.

"You tripping?" she asked, not believing it herself.

His feet started shuffling at the sound of the word, his knees pumping like he was running in place.

"Did you take something?" she asked, bending over him as if he were a small child.

"No, I swear. I only had a Coke."

"Oh God," she said, grabbing him lightly by the chin. "Gunner, somebody was probably trying to do you a favor."

"Oh shit," was all he could say. "Oh shit."

"Listen," Blaze whispered. *Listen.* It was a word she used when she was desperate to be heard. "I'm going to be right here with you." She pointed to the monitor, the little black speaker that fed her voice back to him all night.

"See? Now watch me," Blaze said, pointing to herself so there would be no confusion about who she was.

"Follow me," she said. She had no idea what good that would do. He nodded, a look of profound comprehension.

"Let's do 'When the Levee Breaks'," she said.

"I can do that one," he said, surprise rising in his voice.

"Straight ahead," she said, crawling out from behind the drums.

"Levee," Gunner screamed, barely giving the Vinnys a chance to grab their guitar necks before he counted it off in a hoarse voice. "One, two, three, four." And they were off.

They moved through every fill, every break. With caution they found the verse, the chorus, the bridge, the solo, and when the tricky turnaround came they navigated that too, wobbling through. Careful, careful, Blaze motioned to Gunner. Bring it around. At the end, she motioned him in like a 747, with safety cones and hand signals. Yes, coming home, they were on their way home.

It went on like this for the rest of the night. After the next song, Gunner claimed his sticks were stuck to his hands. He could not lose them. The Vinnys climbed behind the drums and pried them out of his clenched fists. Then after he wiped his hands, they had to tug on the little white hand towel, now hopelessly stuck between his fingers.

During the last half of the set, to occupy him, Blaze danced. For one song, she was a belly dancer. For the next, she did the tango. Even though it was a rock beat, she made it fit. For a while, she directed him like a traffic cop. When the breaks came at the end of the songs, she raised her palm and slashed her neck with her finger to tell him to stop.

For the funky parts, she faked disco moves. And when she got really bored, she unscrewed a cymbal from Bobby Loud's drum set and wore it on her head like a hat. By the end of the night, she had run out of ideas, and then she just resorted to circles, slow and counterclockwise, a dizzy tripping and turning, like dancing around a campfire.

Gunner was rapt. He saw only the traces of things. For the two sticks they all saw hitting the drums, he saw hundreds. He had no idea where the beat was, but he found it. At one point, he stopped the entire band in the middle of the song to compliment the light man on a sweeping progression of lights.

"Excellent!" he yelled from behind the drums as the Vinnys looked on, stunned.

After the final snare snap and tom-tom fill, after the final cymbal crash, they screamed good night to the audience with great relief. The crowd answered with a mild smattering of applause. And with the final chord still ringing in the air, the band went to work dismantling the equipment, returning the guitars to the cases, wrapping all the cords in tight coils and returning them to their heavy black gear boxes.

Blaze took the stairs to retrieve her changes of clothes. Through the course of the night, she had thrown them far and wide in the dressing room. She packed up and walked down the hall to the club owner's office, passing the rows of liquor—Johnson's whiskey, Johnson's tequila, Johnson's gin, rum, and vodka. The bottles were upside down in a pipeline that was connected like an IV to tubes that ran to the bars upstairs.

The tubes gurgled and fed the liquor through the spigots, into the glasses, into all those thirsty mouths—everyone trying to get to that next level. She found the door to the club owner's office. It was open. She knocked, even though she saw him sitting behind his desk.

"Come on in." He waved to her.

He was busy counting money, setting the fives, tens, and twenties out in careful piles with his thick fingers. He was a new club owner, still in his twenties, but already he had that waterlogged, drowning-victim look that club owners so often got from sampling too much of their product.

"I had my doubts about your new drummer right from the start," he said.

She braced herself for what he would say next—I can't bring you back, or I won't pay the contract. She'd heard those lines too many times at the end of a night.

The club owner hesitated for a moment and drew a pile of cash away from the rest of the money. "I don't mind telling you," he said, picking up the wad and counting it again. "I was a real Bobby Loud fan."

"Yeah, well," she stuttered. "That all developed rather quickly just this afternoon—"

"But this sonofabitch is hot," he interrupted. "He's real hot." He handed her the pile of money. She rose and curled the wad into a hard roll in her palm. She smiled and moved toward the doorway, backing out all the way.

Upstairs she found the stage cleared and all the equipment loaded and hauled outside. By now the audience had veered away in their cars, gone home to bad sex or a dead-drunk sleep. Only the dance floor strobing a hopscotch pattern re-called that something had happened there that night.

Outside she found the guys in the band pushing the last piece of equipment into the bus. Bobby Loud was there, too, leaning against the bus with his right foot propped behind him, talking and laughing with Gunner and the Vinnys. His collar was turned up, and an unlit cigarette curled from his lower lip.

"I was all ready to help you out," Bobby Loud said, flicking the lighter and cupping a hand around his smoke. The flame illuminated his beautiful profile. "But those were some serious licks you were playing."

At this Gunner hunched over and began to laugh. He put his big arms around himself and shivered, as if it were too much right now to be in his own body. He leaned against the bus, jangled and giddy.

"No, I'm serious," Bobby Loud said. "That was some bad stuff." All the Vinnys broke out in laughter.

"Yeah, right," Gunner said, his lip quivering. He laughed again and ran his big hands through his hair, which already stood in a straight shock on top of his head. "You want a job?" he said, his eyes wild.

Bobby Loud thought for a while, then said, "Oh, well." He pushed off with his foot. "Why the hell not," he said, heading for the front of the bus.

All of Bad Reputation followed him in a lazy broken line. Gunner and Blaze and all the roadies, all the Vinnys and their tall cool-blond girlfriends climbed one by one into the black-and-red beast that idled and fumed in the dark night, dreaming of the long ride home.

THIS WEEK'S ATTRACTION

Nights off, we go to see Holiday Inn bands. Nicky's mohawk bristles. They make fifteen times what we make, but, oh, those baby blue tuxes and stressed-out cummerbunds.

Nicky sprays on an extra can of White Rain, the sound of hissing from the bathroom. "Yeah," he roars, the windows shaking. "Looks like the damn Statue of Liberty."

I pull on my leather, one long zipper here, one long zipper there. We speed to the freeway in the Nova, not quite orange and not quite red, a blur of rust and muffler.

The lobby is chandeliers and drapery, velvety Muzak and the smell of chlorine from a pool down the hall. On the wall, a map that says, "You are here." We move through the lobby, silver piercings glinting like a constellation.

"The Captain's Cove," a doorman says and points. He's dressed in a tux and tails, a top hat like the coachman from every fairy tale. "Down the hall and to the right."

This week's attraction: on an easel, framed in crushed

velvet, a black-and-white glossy rests at a slant—Four Lords and a Lady. They are laughing, on thrones and wearing tiaras. They throw back their heads for the camera, saying, Let them eat cake.

No surprises, this hotel's motto, from the boardroom to the bedroom to the bandstand. We move through the hallway, punching the blue and yellow balloons on the sign marked "Anderson wedding party."

Inside the Cove, the dark smell of cigarettes and scotch, the swirl of soft chairs and low tables. We spin in circles, order two waters and a double shot of Jack. Nicky follows the waitress to her station, returns with a handful of filberts, maraschino cherries, and green olives.

"Hmmm," he says, popping them in his mouth. "Hors d'oeuvres."

M'lady, we call the vocalist. She wears low-cut black, a shimmer rising from her body. Her voice is dark and muzzled, like NyQuil to our ears.

The Lords are deep into a country medley, plucky guitars and nasal twangs, everything Waylon and Willie. M'Lady shakes her hips and her tambourine. On the dance floor, women in gold shoes hang their arms over the tanned necks of men in golf pants.

The moan of the pedal steel brings the song to a close. In the silence after, we scream, "Hendrix!"

"Did I hear a request?" The guitar player shields his eyes, peers out from the lights.

We duck under the table. "Nine Inch Nails!" we yell. "Play some Ramones!" The pedal steel player warbles a weary lick, the drummer steps deep into his kit, *pa-dumph.*

The bass player, standing off to the left, backs into the darkness. His hair is too long, his Ampeg stack too tall. He pretends to tune his strings, turns to the side, bends over the neck as if listening. In the dark, we see him lift his wrist watch, the Day-Glo green shining eerily on his face. Three more hours to go.

"We're finished here," Nicky whispers. His breath smells of whiskey. "He'll give notice tonight," he says, touching my hand. His fingers are worn thin from practicing. His mohawk spikes tickle my ear.

THE RED-SWEATERED DANCER

She was breaking all the rules, the red-sweatered dancer, with her come-hither looks, and her serpentine steps, and her crooked finger beckoning them onto the dance floor, as if they should drop their guitars, their drumsticks, and surrender to the smooth fluidity of her hips.

In the dressing room during the breaks, they discussed her and all the other dancers—the guy who sank writhing to his knees during the songs and leapfrogged to his feet at the end, the woman in the snug mini who tugged at her hem during the verses and let it ride up her hips during the choruses.

They talked about all the dancers, but mostly they talked about the red-sweatered dancer. They were a band, and so everyone assumed they were anarchists and lowlifes, but they still had a few basic rules of decorum for dancers: no gum popping, no hair tossing, no winking at the band, and no tit shaking. It wasn't a rider in their contract or anything written down. It was just a growing list of don'ts they'd compiled over the year they'd been on the road.

"Is this gonna be our job now?" the lead singer said. His jeans were soft blue and torn at the knee. His face was chiseled and model-rugged. His hair was bleached and trailing down his shoulders.

"If all we're gonna do is spin out these old, familiar tunes," he said and swung at the lampshade, not finishing his sentence—not saying the *then* that should follow the *if*. It was the end of the week, Saturday, and the band was tired, down to the bone.

They'd known they were in trouble on Monday, even before they started, when the waitress started delivering written requests. She set them on the edge of the stage and weighed them down with brimming shot glasses.

Some of the notes were unreadable, sprawled in drunken letters, written on napkins and matchbook covers, requesting well-known songs like "Cocaine" and "Freebird," and even "Wipeout" and "Running Bear." Some of the notes demanded familiar artists like Hendrix, the Doors, and Stevie Ray. The band had no intention of doing those songs. They were working their way across the country, promoting their own music.

The band's name was Darkhorse, and their first CD was called *Young Stallions*. The cover featured a photograph of a herd of wild horses with the band members' faces and upper bodies airbrushed into the horse torsos. Most of the songs on the CD had equestrian themes or, at the very least, a hard-driving beat that sounded like the rapid running of horses' hooves.

Their guitar player wrote the songs late at night while watching old westerns with the mute button on. They hadn't put this all together until they were in the studio and had recorded eight of the twelve tracks, but their CD could have served as a soundtrack to *The Big Trail* or *Cast a Giant Shadow.*

For now they were an unknown band, but someday they hoped to be Darkhorse—one of the names that people wrote on napkins and sent to the stage for bar bands to cover. They knew that playing other people's music wasn't going to get them there.

So Monday had started out bad. Joey, their lead singer, picked up the napkins on the edge of the stage. He cocked his head and let the requests flutter to the ground. "Sorry, don't know that one," he said, throwing back a free shot as if to inflame the audience. Then he picked up the next request, which was written on a book of matches.

"Uh," he said, in a dithering tone. He shook his blond head. "Don't know that one either." Then he ignited the matchbook and flung it onto the dance floor. The flame sputtered and hissed as each match caught fire, then smoldered on the parquet. It was like a gauntlet had been thrown, and no one came near the dance floor.

The drinkers stayed at their tables, pretending not to hear the music. They turned their leather jackets emblazoned with Harley insignias away from the band. They called for the waitresses and ordered drinks, getting more intoxicated and red-faced as the night progressed. All the band could see of them was the backsides of chairs and the long row of orange Harley wings from which loud roars erupted from time to time.

Against the grain of that noise, Darkhorse played, song after song, music of their own making. At the end of each piece, when there was no applause, not even a break in the talking, Joey would hump the mic stand and scream, "Thank you, thank you very much," as if they were the Rolling Stones.

In the noisy space between songs when the lights went down, the band gathered in their own circle on center stage. Pretending to tune their guitars, they leaned into each other and made fun of the crowd.

"Play some Van Halen," they whispered in nasal voices.

"Yeah, man," they said, "let's hear some Eddie."

By the last set on Monday night, the drunken roar became so loud the band couldn't hear themselves talk or play. That's when they turned up, cranked the amplifiers, and screamed louder into their microphones. They had technology on their side—two thousand watts per stack. They were Darkhorse; they *would* be heard.

By Tuesday, all the volume created an audible bulge in the building—too much alcohol and sweat for one room. By Wednesday, the crowd turned ugly. They swung around in their chairs and shouted, "Play some ZZ Top."

The dance floor was long and narrow and surrounded by a wrought iron fence that separated the band from the audience. It was sunken and had roving disco lights and a reflecting mirror ball that rotated overhead. Empty as it was, the dance floor reminded the band of a swimming pool during the lifeguard break—all the anxious swimmers crouching around the edges of the pool waiting for the whistle to blow so they could jump in.

"Play some Nugent," someone shouted. There was a roar of drunken agreement.

"Yeah," a woman with a shrill voice screamed, "play something we can fucking dance to."

And so they had done it. Not because they wanted to, but because it was a long way from Saturday, and Ned, the club owner, had convinced them during the break. "A strictly fiscal decision." He had leaned over and warned them in a voice full of phlegm.

They didn't even have to talk about it. With equipment and truck payments and rent due back home, they would become the human jukebox if necessary.

By Friday they found they had taken on an Ex-Lax regularity, playing the same songs in the same order. They could see the dancers liked knowing what was coming next—so the beautiful girls could abandon the slobs they were dancing with if a slow song was coming, or stay on and dance another if a fast one was next.

By Saturday Darkhorse was emptied of surprises. Their guitar player had taken to wearing the same lopsided hairstyle, which they called a pillow-do. Their bass player wore the same crumpled shirt, which began to smell like sour cream and fried onions. Joey, the lead singer, told the same corny jokes before every song, followed by the drummer's same tired rim shots.

Darkhorse was so bored by Saturday that they had only the dancers to entertain them. During the breaks, they talked about the preppie guy dancing with the older woman in a tight black dress who did the merengue to every song, and they talked about the guy in a leather vest who had tattoos of snakes crawling up his arms. But especially they talked about the red-sweatered dancer.

Since Wednesday, she had been the first one on the floor every night. She danced by herself and moved to a rhythm not of their making. They struggled to match her. Couples came and went, but the red-sweatered dancer stayed on her feet for hours.

Hopeful partners latched on, lurching toward her, but she always lost them, moving in mysterious circles around the floor. She joined in with pairs and formed odd threesomes. She wedged her body between lovers and shook her long dark hair, moving her thin arms in a frenzy.

Darkhorse was terrified of the red-sweatered dancer, especially when she came close to them. She'd migrate to the front of the stage, turn her back to them, and shake her bottom with such ferocity that they were reminded of the final steamy moments of sex.

"I think I saw that on a *National Geographic* special one time," Joey offered during a break.

"Yeah," the guitar player said, wiping his shiny forehead, "it's like some ape mating ritual." The red-sweatered dancer confused the band. They were Darkhorse. Weren't *they* supposed to be the predators?

But every night she disappeared harmlessly. She never spoke to them, just slipped out as they finished playing— retiring, they assumed, to some silky cocoon state where she gathered energy for the next evening.

So they weren't expecting it on the last night when the red-sweatered dancer began to speak to them. At first they couldn't understand her because she shouted while dancing, the words swirling and getting lost in the wake of her movements. She didn't bother to wait for the drummer between songs. She swung her arms and hips and swirled around the waiting dancers.

And it was in this silence between songs that the band finally made out her words. "Play something of your own," she said, moving her body in figure eights. "Play your own music." And as she circled the dance floor, the idea filtered into the hips and arms and feet of all the dancers.

"Yeah." The tattooed guy stomped an iron-toed boot. "Let's hear some of your own stuff."

"Yessss!" The writhing man fell to his knees. He clutched his fists to his chest and screamed, "Let's hear something that's not on the radio."

And so they counted it off—*one, two, three, four*—as the woman in black did the merengue, and Ned, the club owner, sat behind the counter smiling with his sleeves rolled up his big arms. And the red-sweatered dancer spun in irresistible circles, disappearing into the darkness of another Saturday night.

LAST PROM IN HURON, S.D.

There would be other proms, and other bands, the mayor's letter admitted when it reached them, nine months later, bouncing through two scorched-earth time zones and three forwarding addresses. But they would never work in this town again. The letter found the players in winter, too far from last spring, with its baby-blue tuxedos and carnation boutonnieres, for them to remember the details, exactly, of the last prom in Huron, S.D.

The wobble and angle of the mayor's words on faded letterhead reminded them of their flashpots, the burning streamers, and smoke damage to the new gym addition. Then they recalled the blue-and-gold papier mâché staircase—constructed by shop class for the special theme "Stairway to Heaven"—crashing down in flames, the girls with their hair in chignons stomping out the embers in their dyed shoes.

At the time, the players swore to the mayor they would fire their light man, Spike, as soon as they got home, so this could never happen at any other prom in any other town. But they never did. Spike had just returned from a tour with Kiss, running spot on Paul Stanley. He was in possession of certain pyrotechnic skills that made him valuable. In clubs, the band would set the flashpot charge low to miss the ceiling grates. But the gym's high rafters—that place in the cottony clouds where the stairway ended and heaven began— well, it called to them, too.

If only the middle flashpot had blown with the others during the build and kick of "Detroit Rock City." When Spike flipped the switch it was pure beauty—two spirals of gold followed by blue plumes of smoke. A roar went up. Adrenaline rushed through the room.

But that undetonated gunpowder troubled Spike. He stormed the stage, running in front of the band in that scuttling half crouch invented by soldiers and perfected by roadies. And he reset the center fuse so fast that no one noticed.

"Get back," he swung his arms and yelled at the lead singer who preened front and center where he could better see the women in the audience and better be seen by them. The singer was leaned back in a half-scream, his head tilted high with the microphone.

"It's going to blow!" Spike cupped his hands and screamed.

The singer's hips were cocked, his right arm raised in a rock salute, which is just how the flames surrounded him when the flashpot blew, singeing the hair off his right arm and trimming his eyebrows and mustache.

This all may have been disastrous had the singer missed the pickup at the last verse, but he sang through the flames to the smell of burning hair. The band played to the end, feeling they'd escaped catastrophe, which so inspired the second guitarist that he took another solo, and the band followed him as bands must follow a wayward player. So with all the confusion, who would have noticed the streamers rippling in flames, the fire descending the stairway like an angry queen.

Six months later, when the mayor's letter arrived, stamped and bruised in its envelope, they sat around the table and remembered parts of the story: how the drummer leaped from his kit to stamp out flames, but the bassist played on. They remembered how their singer's armpit smoldered, and how happy they were that the sprinklers drenched the rented tuxes and not their rented equipment.

But the one thing the mayor's letter failed to mention, and they themselves had forgotten, was the mayor's daughter, sixteen years old in a red strapless gown, and how she had followed them that night across the state line.

PLAYING FOR THE DOOR

I

They work hard to buy their first electric guitars. They deliver papers or pizzas, mow lawns, or sell magazine subscriptions door-to-door. Their grandparents are disappointed, sure, at first, when they find out the kids have given up the cornet, the tuba, the bass drum, but they agree to match funds to buy their first amplifier. The players agree to pay them back whenever they have the money.

At the music store where they go to buy the equipment, the lady behind the counter winks at their father. The players wonder—does she know something they don't? They practice for months, years, in their bedrooms, in their basements, or at some friend's house whose parents are gone for the weekend. They listen to records and try to make themselves sound just like the person on the record. Sometimes they do, but mostly they sound like themselves trying to sound like someone else.

Eventually they meet a couple of guys at school who have guitars too. One has a mom who's really cool, so she lets the group practice in her basement. They set up their equipment on the cement floor between the washer and dryer, the nautilus machine and the ping-pong table.

Sometimes while they're practicing, their friend's mom comes downstairs to start a load of clothes. She has a high, singing laugh that makes her seem, well, younger. She smokes short French cigarettes and wears short French cigarette pants that show off her ankle bones and the slow, disappearing curve of her bottom as she climbs the stairs.

There's no cool dad in sight, the players notice, but they do not talk about this.

II

That summer their girlfriend decides to throw a sweet-sixteen party in the backyard of her parents' palatial mansion. She also throws a tantrum, locks herself in her yellow chiffon bedroom, makes long-distance phone calls, and smokes roll-your-owns until her parents agree to let the players play.

There's no money involved, but there is free food and all the Coke they can drink. The band only knows eleven songs, but nobody seems to mind. They play the same set over and over, rounding out the hours with their special thirty-five-minute rendition of "Cocaine." The drummer is shirtless; his thin ribs glisten with sweat. The guitar player leans back in his tennis shoes and plays with his tongue hanging out.

Between sets a juggling comedian who also plays the bugle takes the stage. At the first chortle of the horn, the little sisters and brothers stream to the bandstand, ribbons flowing behind them. They are lured away from white ponies and croquet. Sitting in the grass, they watch the red-faced clown as if he were Big Bird.

The players attack the appetizers, palming shrimp canapés and popping them in their mouths like M&Ms. They are not right for the suburbs, they decide. There's too much sunlight and fresh air—no cruel failure or irony here. They need the grit of downtown streets. They need darkness and black leather, brick walls and cigarette smoke around them. Mostly, they wish to suffer.

III

They return to their basement and begin to work up original music in the event that a major recording label happens to seek them out. They learn other songs, too, but are careful not to learn anything that's popular or on the radio at the time.

IV

That fall their older brother hires them for a party in the basement of his frat house. There's no money involved, the brother explains, but there are kegs of beer and plenty of college women roaming around. Early in the night a fist-fight breaks out and their P.A. gets knocked over. Later, after half the plastic cups have been spilled on the floor, the play-ers realize they've set up their equipment directly over the basement floor drain.

As the sludge of Jack Daniels and Budweiser oozes toward them, they lift their sticky feet and take a break to discuss the problem. In a huddle, they vote to risk it all—

the ruin of their shoes, the welfare of their equipment, the possibility of electrocution. Isn't that what Hendrix did at Woodstock?

It's a surly crowd, everyone standing around with button-down shirts and overdeveloped biceps. They don't applaud after the songs, but, the players decide, they're too in awe to clap—the players have so deeply moved them.

V

One of the frat brothers is from a town about sixty miles away, where, he says, there's a club that would be just perfect for the band to play. There's no money involved, you understand, but you could play for the door, and just think of the exposure you'd be getting.

So they rent a P.A. because their last one got toasted at the frat party, and they rent a U-Haul to transport the extra equipment, and their friend's cool mom lends them her Oldsmobile with the hitch on the back.

They get out of town late that day because their drummer is sleeping when they go to pick him up. As they get to the edge of town there's a long, slow train passing through, so just to be kind of rock 'n' rollish they flip off the guy in the caboose as he rolls by. That's when they notice there's no guy in the caboose to flip off anymore.

These big old cars were meant to go ninety, they figure, as they cruise down Highway 10. When the hot light comes on, they assume it's a manufacturer's defect, something their friend's cool mom forgot to tell them about. It's not until later, after they get the equipment unloaded, that they notice a large pool of oil under the car.

VI

The bar is called the Joker's Wild. The club owner has a white shock of hair and a crazy eye that glances randomly at the ceiling as he grabs their hands in his iron grip. After they extricate their picking fingers, numb now and a bit shaken, they wonder if they'll ever play a guitar solo again.

As they set up, stringing cords and checking amplifier levels, country-western songs about cheatin' and fightin' and lovin' and screwin' blare from the speakers above. Slowly the blood returns to their soloing fingers. Buoyed by this, they joke about the crusty old maniac behind the bar, and they decide to change the name of the club to the Owner's Wild.

VII

Before they play, they have a band meeting in the bathroom and decide to take very long breaks and play very short sets. That way, perhaps no one will notice they're repeating every song at least once.

Their drummer, who's obsessed with counting, counts all the people in the club during breaks. He says there are over one hundred people, not counting the comers and goers. At two bucks a pop that makes two hundred bucks, easy. He's busy trying to decide whether he'll buy Paiste or Zildjian cymbals with all the dough they're making.

At the end of the night the owner blinks his crazy eye at the ceiling and reaches under the counter, dipping his shoulder and resting his right palm on what they can only assume is the cherrywood handle of a loaded Derringer. Then he reaches into his left pocket and dumps their cut of the door in a tangled wad of bills on the counter.

The drummer steps forward to count, smooths the bills, all the while tapping his foot in eighth notes on the wood floor. He counts and counts again. Each time it comes out to twenty-five dollars. That makes five bucks each. The owner says it's because (A) they were too loud, (B) nobody liked them, and (C) they're not old enough to be in this club anyway, so they better get the hell out or he's gonna call the sheriff.

They walk to the phone booth on the corner. They call home and ask their dad to come and pick them up. They also ask for twelve hundred bucks to replace the engine in their friend's cool mom's car.

VIII

Here is the story the players know so well because it happened to them. The way their girlfriend didn't mind paying for all the drinks and all the movies and, later, all the motel rooms and all the concert tickets. The way they drove around in her sporty coupe, all the time pretending that her car belonged to both of them.

They remember the job at Burger King or Pizza Hut or K-Mart, where they started working to pay off their relatives. How the shifts cut into their practice time and the night manager watched them like a hawk because they were musicians and he thought they might (A) be on drugs, (B) try to steal something, or (C) try to get out of working Friday and Saturday nights.

They remember how their dad kept a comfortable distance from them because he knew if he was too friendly to them at any given moment, the players would ask him for more money. And the way that everyone in the band quit, one by one, and was replaced by others who quit, always for the same reason—no money, and eventually, man, you've got to do something with your life.

IX

They probably remember best the way their friends laughed that nervous kind of laugh when they asked what the players were planning to do when they grew up. The friends, who had gone to college and acquired jobs, families, and houses, knew they were being cliché, but still, they wanted to know.

Finally, the players noticed that all those guys in IBM commercials had nice-looking wives waiting for them in cushy condos, and as they navigated slippery mountain roads in their sports cars talking on their cell phones, they never once appeared to be gazing at a hot light. So they went back to school and changed their majors from music or art to business or marketing, with a computer science minor.

How about the way they winked at the lady behind the counter of the music store when they sold their equipment back to her? Or the way they still go to nightclubs with their lovely wives and tell stories about their many years as a musician—the details growing dimmer, the stories growing sweeter with each telling.

THIS NEW QUIET

The day after the fire, all their equipment charred in a ditch and blown to ashes, the thin axle of the truck lying on its side like the burned-out frame of a dragonfly, they gathered in a living room on a circle of old couches. The players sat forward, their eyes studying the swirls in the worn carpet.

They who had the power to make so much noise sat in this new quiet. They did not speak of debt or creditors, nor did they speak of lost guitars—the blond Les Paul, and the mahogany Gibson double-neck that sang sweetly in its velvet case as it rolled down the highway.

They sat in silence, trying to find the new words the fire had left on their tongues. Outside traffic rushed by, the clatter of passing trains, the honk of angry horns, as the sun dialed its way around the room and disappeared.

In the half dark someone stood. It was the tall blond guitar player who rose, wobbly in his black boots. He stood in the center of the spiral, raised his thin hands to his face and blew out one long exhale. It hissed through the room like a wild balloon losing steam.

When all the wind was out of him, he gulped one deep breath, swung a long arm like a knockout punch through the sheer emptiness of air, and said, *Fuck.* It was only one word. It was inadequate for the moment. But it was a good place to start.

THE HALF-LIFE OF THE NOTE

Madison has been stealing purple clothes. This is how she does it. She goes into stores with her three small daughters. "Only browsing," she says, complimenting the salesgirl on her earrings. She invites the woman to pat the baby's fuzzy head.

Madison circles the store, baby stroller bumping through the aisles.

"I'm looking for an outfit," she tells the woman, talking loud like someone who owns cars and houses. "Something to wear to San Francisco for my husband's medical convention."

"Cardiology," she says, ferreting through the displays, sliding the hangers along the aluminum rack. The outfit she chooses is an expensive rayon jersey two-piece. It comes in three colors, one of which is purple.

"Oh, poo," she tells the salesgirl. She can't decide which shade she likes best, and it appears she has forgotten her color wheel at home. "I guess I'll have to try them all," she sighs. "I'm not sure if I'm an eight this week, or a ten."

Madison (not her real name) confesses this to Kinky Salazar (also not her real name) one night after Madison has put her three small daughters to bed and the two women are standing in her walk-in closet admiring all the purple things she has so larcenously acquired.

"This, I got at Von Maur," Madison says, lifting an eyebrow and pulling out a twinkling amethyst dinner jacket with sequins and pearls running along the edges.

Kinky Salazar is staying with Madison for a few weeks, waiting for her new band to worm their way along the circuit and pick her up. So far she's received reports from Columbus and Cincinnati, Indianapolis, and Chicago. Soon they'll reach Kansas City. But before she shoves off, Madison wants her advice: Does this go with that? And doesn't she agree that when Madison finds her own band, she'll be in pretty good shape, clothingwise?

Kinky Salazar is eyeing the door. These days she assesses her own level of comfort in a room by its number of exits. The walk-in closet is well-lit and neat, no funky shoe smells. Soft tan carpet. Track lighting. Every piece of clothing has its own place, nothing draped over the top of something else. Still, Kinky feels nervous. Madison looms large between herself and the only exit.

So this will be the story tonight, Kinky thinks. Two nights before, she heard about the time a prowler broke into the apartment. Madison was hunched in the darkness at the top of the landing, waiting for the last possible moment until the vague outline of the prowler's body, the muscular biceps and the moisture of his breath, were almost upon her. Then she threw her body weight at him, using gravity, toppling him backward down the stairs. Kinky was skeptical, but Madison showed her the shock of blood-crusted black hair, torn from his scalp, that she keeps in her jewelry box. Downstairs, Kinky's astonished fingers traced the crowbar jimmy marks on the front doorframe.

"Nobody comes near my kids," Madison said, flashing a she-bear look.

Last night, Kinky heard all the details and locations of Madison's three home births. The first two were upstairs, with midwives; the last one was downstairs, alone. Madison lay on the living room carpet, pulling the bloody, nameless thing from herself.

Kinky Salazar has no children. She cringes at the sight of blood. In high school health class, when they showed the wonders-of-childbirth movie, she was the one who went limp and white-faced and had to leave the room.

"So," Madison says, twirling around the walk-in closet with her new stolen purple rayon jersey two-piece. "I tell the salesgirl I'm really interested in accessorizing." She stands in front of the mirror, framing her face with a matching plum-colored silk blouse. "That really gets their creative juices flowing."

So this is how Madison does it. She takes the baby into the dressing room, stroller and all. She gets two or three saleswomen working for her, running back and forth exchanging sizes and colors, so no one remembers whose customer she is. She bends their minds like cheap spoons in the direction of brooches, earrings, and matching hose. To complicate things, she instructs her two toddlers to play in the hallway just outside the dressing room.

She gets these saleswomen doing the goose-step. They are flinging coordinates over the curtain, all the time reminding her about the twenty-five percent markdown on everything in the store. The saleswomen trip over Madison's two small daughters, who are guarding the dressing room door like peachy-faced infantry.

Inside, with clothes raining down on her, Madison feigns interest, answering "uh, huh" and "oh, really" to all their comments, as she slips one more purple garment inside the stroller under the baby's well-powdered bottom.

"This one was nearly impossible to get," she says to Kinky, holding a one-piece magenta catsuit up to her body. She waits for Kinky's nod of approval. "They had security in that store like Alcatraz."

Kinky nods, pretending to listen. She's thinking about how she has three more days before Nicky & the Slashers come to pick her up. "We are coming soon to abduct you." That's how Nick put it on the phone when he called her from Pittsburgh to tell her she had the job.

She was between gigs when she answered the ad that said, *Working rock band looking for an extra hand and a soprano voice.* She didn't know what to make of the "extra hand" requirement—what could that mean? "I sing with great force and keep my hands to myself," she wrote on a piece of paper, which she slipped in the mail with a photo and a tape. Her instincts were right. They wanted someone to play two-bit keyboard parts and sing background vocals while swinging and swaying in a tight-fitting black dress, slit-to-the-clit.

"Your tape sounded great," Nick of Nicky & the Slashers said to her the first time he called. She could hear some reservation in his voice.

"But?" she said, waiting for the rest.

"But we did some checking."

"Yeah?" Kinky said, holding her breath for what might come next.

"Well, we heard you wear a machete on stage."

"Oh that," Kinky crooned into the receiver. "That was a long time ago." Then, she added, when Nicky remained silent, "and in Montana." Almost another country. They couldn't refuse her. She had the voice—three and a half octaves. She had the dress and the body to go with it.

Kinky Salazar's life: Madison wants it. And the singer would almost hand the mess over to her, trade it for Madison's own mess—the three daughters, the monthly welfare check, even the rusty Chevy that drips oil in the driveway and starts every third try.

"When the Slashers come," Madison says, "I could pretend I'm you."

Why steal something so worthless? Kinky wants to ask. Better to filch a wardrobe. That way, if the life comes along, you'll have something to wear to it.

"Here's the thing," Kinky says finally, standing in the walk-in closet, the track lighting heating the small space. "The life itself will never stand up to the dream of the life."

Madison holds up a mauve chiffon tea-length dress. "This one looks really nice on." She binds it around her waist to give Kinky the total effect. "Kind of romantic."

It does look nice. Madison is a beautiful woman, darkly handsome, large bones, brown eyes, an open, trusting face. But maybe it's too open—a greenhorn look that the people in her business who make a living using other people would recognize as a willingness to do whatever is necessary.

At thirty-two Kinky is an old woman in her profession. She's long past desperate. But when she looks in the mirror, she doesn't fear the traces of wrinkles or the occasional gray hair as much as she fears the recurrence of a born-to-sell-cheeseburgers look. Over the years she has cultivated a dark hollowness in her face that says in a glance, "I am no one you would care to fuck with."

Madison's eyes are like sponges, little detail collectors. All week Kinky has withstood the constant perusal, the study and absorption of all her movements, mannerisms, and vocal inflections.

All week Kinky has felt Madison's attention pass over her body like a delicate probe, reviewing, reviewing. One day she hears herself say something about music—the mix is wet, the bass sound is aggressive, the singer's voice is sandpaper sweet—and the next day she hears a facsimile of the phrases play back from Madison's mouth, copied off her like guitar licks off an album.

It's not about stealing things, Kinky Salazar wants to say, or about collecting more. These words stay nestled deep in the hollow of her mouth. It's about letting things fall from you. All week she has wanted to spit these words out like something bitter and used up. But when she's tried, they've come out garbled. And she's never been able to get to the last part: how once things begin to let go, there's no way of stopping them.

"Go and sit on the bed and close your eyes," Madison orders Kinky like a mother orders a child. In her house, it's difficult to disobey. Madison pulls a fuchsia cowboy hat from the top shelf of the closet and tucks the brim down below her eyes. She grew up in the west. The hat must be from her rodeo days.

"Go on, now," she says, turning Kinky by the shoulders. "I'll be right out."

Kinky sighs and sits down hard on the bed like a disgusted child. Every day at Madison's house is show-and-tell—tonight it's a rope coiled on the floor like a sleeping snake and a kerchief tied loosely around her neck, cowpoke-style. Tonight it's spit-polished cowboy boots and a stiff Stetson, gentlemanly tipped as Kinky opens her eyes.

Madison stands in her bedroom and picks up the rope in a slow, dramatic fashion, twisting the knotted end in her palm. She begins to sing in a low voice that pulls and aches from deep in her belly, a voice dark and hoarse that sounds like the beginning of laryngitis, but is Madison's own natural voice.

> *Sixty-six and ninety-nine had to meet that day*
> *Some say it was the luck of the draw*
> *The meannest cowboy ever born*
> *And the stubbornest horse you ever saw*

She sings it with real passion, not with a country twang but in a thick, mournful voice. There are twenty-some verses, Kinky counts, all going on endlessly telling this tale of symbiosis, about this ride to the death—the twisting, the bucking, the gyrations, and the dust in their mouths. The cowboy hangs on as the horse tries to free itself from its burden, the cowboy's left arm flapping high in the air with each jolt.

Madison sings on, twisting and twirling the rope. *It's a pity, a darn pity,* she pauses for the last verse, singing it slow and drawn out, savoring each word. The horse has broken its own back from bucking. The cowboy stays with the beast until the end, until the men come to shoot it. When it's over, Madison sniffs and lowers her hat.

Kinky can feel him in the hallway, sliding his hands along the dark walls later that night when everyone is sleeping and the house is quiet. She wakes and knows there's a man in the house. Kinky thinks about the three children sleeping in the room across the hall, but then she hears him in Madison's room—rummaging, the slight creak of the bed, some faint talking.

Soon the knocking begins, the headboard's rhythmic touch against the wall. Kinky wills herself to sleep. Through the thin wallpaper, Madison's breath takes him in, the steady pulse, the hoarse gasps. Later there is light laughter, the dark silence of sleep.

In the morning, before breakfast, he's gone. Kinky comes into the kitchen in her bathrobe and looks around the room. No one there but Madison fixing breakfast. She wonders if she's imagined him.

"I can't stand him during the day," Madison admits. "He smells of car grease, and he doesn't know how to dress."

"Well," Kinky says, "he must do something right."

"Ah," Madison says, waving a spatula, "he's got great

hands." She turns and smiles.

They talk in the kitchen while Madison fixes omelets. She's chopping onions, casual with the knife, like one who has handled cutlery for a long time. Kinky never takes up a kitchen knife. In the past when she's done so, she's been told she looks dangerous. She doesn't want to scare the children.

Soon the kitchen becomes populated. The baby is in the high chair banging her bowl. "Juice," she says, her small teeth forcing out the small word, *juice*. Simple requests. The two toddlers mill around Madison's feet.

"Yes, yes," Madison answers. She's easy with her children. They hang from her hips like ripe fruit as she stirs pancake batter. They are well-behaved kids, well-trained. They never push Madison and they don't whine.

Perhaps it's her choice of bedtime entertainment. Last night they listened to Pink Floyd's *The Wall*. As Madison stood in the middle of the living room singing along—*what shall we use to fill the empty spaces*—her little ones sat on the couch watching her with eyes wide open. Her voice sounded eerie, as if asking who will be the pestle and who the mortar.

There's something military about Madison, Kinky realizes. Her children obey her like soldiers. When she puts them down to sleep, they stay down. They're not messy kids. They put their toys back in the wicker basket.

There's no dust on Madison's shelves, no knickknacks. In her drawers, no half-burnt candles rolling around, no long-expired coupons twisted in with the silverware. In the cupboards, no fifty-year-old casserole dishes from Grandma with chips around the side. Nothing in this house is over a year old. Relic that she is, Kinky wonders what she's doing here.

"My period is late," Madison says the next morning cutting green peppers. She opens the refrigerator and pulls out the milk carton. "That son of a bitch grease monkey," she says, lowering her nose into the spout to smell the milk. "He told me he was shooting blanks." This is Madison's way of saying that she can't afford another child.

Appetite, Kinky Salazar thinks. The word has been running through her head like the lyrics of a song she can't remember. There is something about appetite that she meant to tell Madison before she left. Something about losing appetite—how you must let your taste for the things of the world fall away from you.

"Sometimes I dream about what it would be like to sing in a band," Madison says, setting down the chopping knife. She sits at the kitchen table and lets the pans steam on the stove behind her. "To travel from town to town like you and not have to worry about anything," she says, looking straight at Kinky.

Madison admits this to Kinky Salazar one morning a few days before Nicky & the Slashers are scheduled to arrive. She admits it while chopping green peppers and onions, with her babies hanging from her hips. She admits it, handling the knife casually, two weeks late for her period.

Kinky wonders how many people know where she is. Only Nicky & the Slashers, and what do they know? She hasn't spoken to her family in over two years. Too many arguments about this life. Eventually she stopped calling. The same went for men. She was free and unaccounted for.

And what did she know about Madison? A friend of a

friend, really. "She's a little crazy," their one common friend Rita had warned her. At the time she'd thought Rita meant funny-crazy or party-crazy or sex-crazy. What's the big deal? she'd thought. Everyone she knew was at least two kinds of crazy. "She's nice up front," Rita said, "but watch your back."

Watch your back. That's what Kinky meant to tell Madison before Nicky & the Slashers came to pick her up.

Madison. She had found the name one night while watching a black-and-white movie. There was an old theater in the movie with double glass doors and swirls of brass handles. Up above was the marquee, hundreds of lights all pulsing together to form the name, "The Madison."

"You named yourself after a movie theater?" Kinky says, lifting her voice high at the end.

"The name of avenues, cities, and presidents," Madison says with a winsome twist of the lips. Soon she plans to see and be all of these.

"I wanted a name that would roll off the tongue," she explains. "Like if you went to the record store and said to the guy with the long hair behind the counter, 'Do you have the latest Madison album,' he would actually get off that stool and go to the racks and find it for you."

The two women laugh. Kinky thinks of all the incense-filled head shops she's been in, with the records in the front and the pipes in the back. Always at the front counter you had the thin-armed waif with the nose ring who so intimidates you with her disdain that you vow to buy something that will impress her. You search around—the tapestry on the walls, the carved wood boxes, and in a glass case near the back of the store, all those delicate glass pipes and bongs.

When she first started out, Kinky haunted these record stores, searching through the racks to see the names of all the new bands. She herself had gone through a fair share of stage names. She'd tried the catchy names (Lizzie Borden, Typhoid Mary) and the corny names (Pearl Harbor, Patty Link Sausage—that one from a band where everyone was named after a cut of meat). She even tried the one-name names (Estelle, Jamaica). None of them was quite right.

"How did you get *your* name," Madison asks.

"A few years ago on a plane from Chicago to New York," Kinky explained. "A married dude kept hitting on me. There was a lot of wine and talk about meeting in the bathroom." The two women laughed out loud. "He gave me his card and told me to call him, but I took his name instead."

Madison scowls at this explanation. "Couldn't you just say your mother met your father at a bullfight?"

"It's only a name," Kinky says.

"Well, it's an *okay* name, but you need a better story," Madison explains. "You need a bio that will make people say things like 'Salazar is a rock-and-roll meteor dropped to earth'."

"Please," Kinky says, feeling her face heat up. "I don't think anybody would ever say that." *Between gigs*—that's how she would describe herself. She's a woman with good hair, lungs as powerful as a snowblower, two suitcases full of black leather clothes, and a knack for sleeping well in moving vehicles. The thing that's kept her going all these years is a tic in her brain, a throb at her throat, the sharp breeze of something unnameable at her back.

"You're only as good as your last performance," her high school band teacher used to say with enthusiasm.

"Uh, excuse me, Mr. Sullivan," she's imagined herself calling him up in the middle of the night all these years later. Maybe she'd have had a few shots of tequila. "You're only as good as whoever remembers your last performance." A subtle distinction, but important.

The half-life of the note, how it exists only in the foggy universe of memory, has always troubled her. Even the best-sung, most rarefied notes are destined to dissipate as soon as they hit the atmosphere of the real world. Painters end up with paintings, poets with books to remind them of their efforts. But words sung and unsung, everything born on the breath, is destined to ride that steady curve down into nothingness.

There were a few select moments she'd nurtured. That one night in Grand Island, no one in the audience but some guy with a cigar sitting at the bar complaining about how it's too loud, how it's never this loud at the Holiday Inn. And she, looking at the little space between his eyes, thinking how she'd like to drive a spike right through him, and *wham*, this note comes out of her so perfect it almost makes a clean cracking sound like a bat hitting a home run.

And there was the time driving across Idaho to get to Boise before morning. Four a.m. No one awake but rattlesnakes and coyotes. Then driving on Highway 86, foothill after foothill, the truck straining to rise along the incline, and the feeling that the whole thing might run away on the way back down. Both her feet on the brake, the weight of the equipment lurching at her back, and then finally hitting the plateau, the stars coming out, and the high pitch that had been ringing in her ears suddenly gone. And the Snake River snaking along, and she along with it, and that song coming on the radio—*I can hear it calling me the way it used to do*—and she, finally understanding what *it* might possibly mean. But these were rare, intangible moments.

"Everyone changes their name for the stage," Madison is saying. She's sitting at her dressing table brushing her hair. "Even Hitler," she says. She drapes her bangs over one eye like Streisand in *Funny Girl*.

There are no lighted mirrors where you want to go, Kinky wants to say. *And no babies*. She wants to shake Madison. There's no room for babies out there.

On those long night drives, she's imagined herself as a frontierswoman exploring virgin territory. For a woman to survive on the road, she must be tough, self-reliant, willing to make sacrifices. It's the only hedge against the half-life of the note.

Madison is sitting at the mirror, purple maribou slung around her shoulders. She's practicing the application of false eyelashes. "When Salazar sings," she winks at Kinky, "people listen."

"Good night," Kinky says, turning to go. She can't take any more. At the very least, Madison has perfected the art of hyperbole. Kinky pauses at the door, looks back. Madison is surrounded by feather boas, vials of perfume, and makeup.

"Just like they used to say about those old jazz singers," Kinky says, looking back. She raises her wine glass to toast the host. "When Madison sings a song, it stays sung."

✦

Madison is steaming. It's early morning and she's been to the all-night grocery. There's been a fight with the manager over trading stamps.

"I paid the bill," she fumes, and slams down the contents of the bag. Diapers, formula, frozen carrots and peas, toilet paper appear on the counter. "I had the stamps in my hand." She pauses as if trying to reconstruct her steps. "And when I went outside, the wind blew them right out of my hand." Madison pulls open the freezer and begins to stack orange juice and pork chops wrapped in white paper. The baby is on the floor gnawing at the corner of the saltines box.

"And when I went inside to ask for replacement stamps," Madison says into the freezer, teeth gritted, "he didn't believe I had lost them." A cloud rises around her head. "It was five seconds later, and the son of a bitch wouldn't believe me."

So she punched him. Then the manager called the cops and filed assault charges against Madison, mother of three, possible mother of more, coveter of trading stamps. All this before 8 A.M.

Kinky has heard enough. She wants to go to her room. She has just taken care of three children for one hour. She is exhausted. She feigns a yawn and rises to go.

"No," Madison says, "don't go." She puts out her hand and sits down at the kitchen table. "Sometimes I just feel like giving up." She buries her face in her arms. "Did you ever want something so bad?"

"Sure," says Kinky, patting Madison's hand. She's still thinking about the trading stamps. At one time she wanted everything. When she was twenty-one, she and her boyfriend would lie in bed after making love and talk about how they were going to have fourteen babies.

It was hormones talking, but one night lying in the candlelight, they calculated on their fingers and toes the number of eggs she had left, up to the age of forty. The number was 247 then, and it was less than half that now.

Madison pulls the baby onto her lap. The toddlers are patting her arms, patting her legs, stroking her hair. "Sometimes I just feel like handing them over to someone," she says, dabbing her eyes with a tissue. Kinky wonders how much of this the girls can understand. She imagines that someday they'll tell their psychoanalysts about this morning.

"Sometimes," Madison pauses, blowing her nose and whispering, "I get afraid I might hurt them."

Kinky sees now that staying here has been a mistake. Her presence confuses things. Instead of the lonely life Kinky actually lives, Madison sees some wild ride. Madison does not see all that Kinky has dropped along the way—family, friends, not to mention her 143 (at last count) eggs that have been spread across the continent, wasted.

Even her sense of humor is gone. Near as she can tell, she lost it somewhere between Salt Lake City and Provo, going south on I-15. At first the change was subtle, like gaining a few pounds—all of a sudden everything starts to feel tight. She imagines it happens just like in those Gold Card commercials: the busy executive leaves his briefcase on top of a rented sedan. He gets in and speeds away. In the burnoff of squealing tires, the briefcase smashes to the ground, and all those infinite lines of credit spill out onto the pavement, irretrievable. Kinky is hoping that Nicky & the Slashers are going west. She's considered searching the ditches.

Madison sits quietly weeping at the table. The ice cream and peas defrost on the counter.

"C'mon," Kinky says, and pulls Madison to her feet. "I'll watch the girls."

After Madison goes to her bedroom, Kinky picks up the downstairs extension and calls her new band at their motel in Peoria. The ring goes on and on. It sounds far off and distant, like she's calling another country.

"Nicky, dude," she whispers, trying to sound casual when he finally picks up. In the background she can hear the sound of a television, a blow dryer, a woman laughing. She wonders how many people she'll have to clear out of the way to make her place in the band.

She prefers guitarists. It's not a matter of love or even desire. In three weeks, she'll be sleeping with Nick of Nicky & the Slashers. In five weeks, she'll be telling Adolpho, the lead singer, to move over. In two months, she'll be using all three and a half octaves. She'll be a full Slasher, no longer an accessory. The takeover will be amicable; she won't even need a machete.

"Just wondering if you forgot about me," Kinky breathes into the receiver. She uses the soft part of her voice.

"Never baby, never," Nicky says in a hoarse voice, maybe a little drunk. "We could never forget you," he says, and it sounds ridiculous even to her, since they've never even met.

Picture your body blooming like a weapon, she thinks. That's something else she meant to tell Madison before she shoves off.

✦

Madison has been giving living room performances. It happens in the afternoons when the truants from the high school have a few hours to kill before they can go home. They come to Madison's house for a beer and a joint and a bit of homemade music. Most days it's Madison performing her strange, unearthly tunes. She stands tall behind her keyboard, going into a trance like a high priestess spouting liturgy.

Music for Narcoleptics is the working title of her unrecorded album. It features rambling one-note synth lines that sound like Gregorian chant run through a handheld band saw—now moaning, now plunging low, now screeching to supersonic levels.

One day Kinky brought out her guitar to jam, but she found that Madison was impossible to accompany. She didn't know the minor scale, she didn't know the major scale. She only knew this wild wailing inside her head and the schizophrenic scat that went with it. *Plastic yellow / plastic yellow clouds / I know you're hiding the real sun / covering up my windows today / get that fake sun away / away from me.*

"Whoa, man," one of the truants bounces in his seat and whispers, "that's deep." He flips his long bangs out of his eyes.

When she tires of performing her own work, Madison turns on the stereo and breaks out her Mr. Microphone. She paces the room, lip-synching to Nina Hagen's guttural German rendition of "White Punks on Dope." Then she puts on the live version of "Highway Star" and plays air guitar to the ten-minute solo. She leans back and manipulates her fingers along an imaginary neck, kneeling on one knee, grimacing along with the sixteenth notes.

After she's really warmed up, she circles the room as if this were Vegas and she were Eydie, and then she sings Patti Smith passionately *(because the night belongs to lovers)*, finishing up with Pat Benatar. Eventually she makes her way to Kinky, who is crouching in the space between the stereo and the TV.

"Well, Ms. Salazar," Madison says, leaning over her like a quiz show host, "here's a chance to practice your chops."

"Oh no," Kinky says, waving her hand. "I only sing for money."

Madison is unfazed. She moves on, leans over a tipsy teenager. "You're a heartbreaker," she whimpers, blowtorching the *h*. She takes the teen by his needle-haired chin, as if she's entertaining the troops, and sings, "Dream maker, love taker, don't you mess around with me." The living room crowd loves her. She gets lots of applause, rave reviews.

Well, she's ready for the Holiday Inn, Kinky thinks later that night as she packs her bags. Nicky & the Slashers are due to arrive the next morning and Kinky wants to be in the driveway, ready to throw her bags in the back of the van.

Madison comes into the bedroom as Kinky folds her clothes into the suitcase. "What did you think," she asks Kinky. She lies down on the bed and fingers the nubby bedspread.

"You had them eating out of the palm of your hand," Kinky says, trying to think of something constructive to say. Madison hangs on her words.

"What does it matter what I think?" Kinky says. "I'm no

fine example." And besides, in a week the whole thing will be just more grist for the story mill anyway, tailored to Madison's fictions. Kinky can almost taste it. This is one of those moments in life that gets away from you, produces ravenous offspring.

She remembers the time when she drank one shot of Quervo with some guy in a bar in Topeka. The next time she went back to Kansas, he's at the bar asking her, does she remember that time they downed a whole bottle?

Kinky doesn't worry about it. For a rock singer any promo, even bad promo, is good for you. People expect you to misbehave. She never discourages a little fictionalizing.

Madison picks up a black leather bustier from Kinky's suitcase. "Can I try this on?" she asks, sitting up.

Kinky pulls out the matching skirt—black leather and shorter than short. Her old guitar player used to say it unplugged his sinuses when she wore it.

"Go ahead," she tells Madison, digging for the chunky leather belt and spiked wrist bands.

Madison goes to her bedroom and changes. "Ready?" She stands outside in the hallways, as if it were an unveiling.

"Ready," Kinky says.

Madison rounds the corner and enters Kinky's room like she's stepping on stage. Of course, she's violently beautiful in black leather. Her long arms are sleek; her bare shoulders are muscular. She spins in circles, then sits down on the bed. In black leather, she exudes readiness—the sweet odor of sex.

"Everyone tells me how I've made my bed," Madison says, running her fingertips over the metal spikes of the wristband, "and now I should lie in it." She smiles at Kinky tenderly, then leans over and kisses the singer deep on the lips.

Kinky leans in, then leans back when she feels the tips of the metal spikes on her neck. She breaks the kiss. "Tomorrow," she says to Madison, "men will be coming for me."

"Oh, poo," Madison says, getting off the bed. She swings her arms wide in a whirl of chains and leather. "I still wish it was me going tomorrow instead of you."

He is standing in the doorway in the middle of the night. The unnatural stillness wakes Kinky. The hush of someone watching, holding his breath, causes her to start out of bed.

She has dreamt about the knife again. This time she's surrounded by surgeons who trace a neat path along her belly with a scalpel, opening her like a can of smoked oysters. She sits up in bed, shakes her head and tries to concentrate on the dimly lit face in the doorway. Before her eyes can focus, he's gone. By the time she gets out of bed, she can hear he's scuttled down the steps and out the door.

Kinky follows the light to the bathroom. In the bathtub and the sink, she finds streaks of blood—dark, viscous pools of maroon.

She thinks first of the children, then she turns and rushes to the girls' bedroom. Inside she finds them tousled in sleep, rosy and warm in their bunk beds. The baby breathes lightly in the crib. Even though it's the middle of the night, the baby is awake. She's not crying, just gazing up with an open-infant trust. Kinky leans over in the dark and lifts her out of the crib.

She walks through the dark room with the baby in her

arms, smoothing the strands of soft hair. She cups the baby's tender head, fragile as an egg in her palm. She walks down the hallway with the baby and checks the master bedroom. Inside, Madison is lying awake on her bed, a large white towel pinned around her torso.

"It's a mess, I know," she says when Kinky walks in. Madison's skin is drawn and colorless except for the dark nipples that spread in wide circles like pinches of nutmeg on the whiteness of her breasts.

"It's going to be okay," Madison says to Kinky, smiling weakly. "The grease monkey took care of everything."

Kinky sits on the bed, clutching the baby to her body, the warmth like a small furnace on her shoulder.

Madison reaches up and runs a finger lightly down the baby's tiny back. "Someday," she says, her voice trailing off as she looks toward the window, "I'm going to get out of this place." Her profile is sharp, and as she says the words, a chill runs through Kinky.

The singer rises from the bed and turns to leave the room. The day's first light seeps through the window. Outside, the horizon is turning a bruised pink and blue. Kinky cannot seem to put the baby down. She wants to keep her hands pressed always around the child's tender head. There will be no more sleep for her tonight. She talks softly to the baby as she goes down the stairs.

Once in the kitchen, she straps the infant in the high chair, talking to the baby about everything she's doing— see, now I'm unloading the dishwasher, now I'm fixing your formula. The baby watches her move around the room like the most attentive audience she's had in years. Kinky sets the table for breakfast, putting out the bowls and spoons and the girls' favorite cereal. She has learned all their preferences over the last two weeks.

After this is finished, she walks back upstairs, returning the baby to her soft crib. In her own room, Kinky makes the bed one last time and zips her suitcases shut. As quietly as possible, she manhandles the suitcases down the stairs, noticing they are overpacked and too heavy. She takes them outside and sets them on the stoop.

For a long time, she sits on the front steps and watches the sun as it tries to break through the envelope of the horizon. Even now she can almost see the top fringe of the dawn breaking through the trees. She sits in the silence before morning and thinks about the headlights of a truck—those twin meteors racing madly toward her in the night.

THE GUITAR PLAYER
RUNS OUT OF IDEAS

Jam Session, Saturday afternoon. Somewhere between the nicotine poison of Friday and the drop dead sleep of Sunday, somewhere between hung over and strung out, the players gather at the 4-10 Lounge, early afternoon, before the strippers come to start their shows.

In the club, the ashy odor of last night's smokes and the yeasty mash of beer. The bathroom doors are propped open with garbage cans, and the toilet seats are up. The water's blue, but the air still smells of piss and pot.

The owner wears an apron behind the bar. He runs a damp white cloth over the counter. Free crock pot chili in plastic bowls. But mostly the players come to hear each other.

A guitar player's on stage, wearing a mad hatter hat under dim house lights. He's doodling licks to the bass and drums, stranded deep in the wrong key. When he tries to right himself, heads go up, ears tweak. Get in the box, pal, someone yells.

A few tables are full—people who've come out to see the players. Friends, and friends of friends. A couple wanders in off the street, drinking and fighting for hours. I did *not* touch your sister, the man says to the woman. They take the dark corner table.

The guitar player has run out of ideas. His Les Paul is slung low on his hips. He stomps his pedal with his boot, leans over his axe like a lover, coaxes the G-string high. It breaks loose and bounces in the light like an unruly strand of hair.

The other players sit around with their cases open. They've been tuning and running scales for half an hour. He'll be off soon enough, they know from experience. He'll either run out of strings or neck.

The guitar player's D-string wobbles low. He plucks the tuning pegs between licks. *De-da-la, de-da-la, de,* he plays, grasping for ideas. Where did things go so wrong?

His face is bent in concentration, a cigarette smoldering from his lips. *De-da-la, de-da-la, de,* he plays again. He plants his feet on the X of duct tape where the spotlight shines the brightest.

The Hunger Bone

When Sal got back to his motel room, he pulled his guitar from the case and began to practice. Some men came home to their wives and some to their guitars. It was late afternoon. The sun was beginning to set. He still had a few hours to kill before the rest of the band came knocking on his door to tell him it was time to go play.

He propped himself on the edge of his motel room bed—so like all the beds from all the weeks before—and he began to practice, playing scales and riffs, losing himself to the repetition. And just as his hands returned to the same strings and frets, so his mind returned to Mr. Brecker.

What Sal remembered most about Mr. Brecker, even hours after the meeting, was the shiny spot on the top of his head. Not a bald spot, really, just a thinning spot that the man had worried with his long fingers as they talked, returning to it again and again, as if hoping it may have disappeared.

Sal's supervisor, Jack Kelly, was with him on the sales call. They spent the afternoon sitting around a dining room table trying to convince Mr. Brecker to buy a headstone for his wife, who had died two weeks earlier of an inoperable brain tumor.

Sal hadn't done any talking at the table; he had merely *observed.* That's the word Jack Kelly used to get him in the door after Mr. Brecker opened to their knock, looking confused, wringing his hands at the sight of two salesmen, instead of the one he had been expecting.

"Anything, even the slightest thing, can throw these people off," Jack Kelly had warned him on the way to the meeting. "Grief is a delicate business." He cranked the steering wheel and sent his station wagon bouncing into Mr. Brecker's driveway.

And that was when Sal knew that Jack Kelly hadn't swung by Sal's motel room, five hundred miles off of his normal sales route, just because he missed his ugly face, as he'd said. Instead, Sal realized, Jack Kelly was there to give him a re-treading—the company's last-ditch effort to salvage a salesman before taking away his territory.

When they finally got into Mr. Brecker's house, Jack wasted no time. Within moments he had the product samples out on the table, small heavy rectangles of granite and marble from around the world—pink pearl, Dakota mahogany, Kashmir white, paradise black.

"Yes, sir," he said cheerfully. "This Costa Rican carnelian is really hard to come by." He stretched his jaw into a smile. Sal remembered the training session on how to smile at customers, and he saw that Jack Kelly's was the perfect salesman smile—so open, trusting, and delighted to be talking about product that you hated to see it disappointed.

"In this business, son," Jack had told him at lunch, "you either grow a thick skin, or you lose it." Sal had listened with interest. In the few months he'd been working for the company, he hadn't sold a single chip, block, or headstone of rock. And wasn't as if he hadn't tried.

Sitting in Mr. Brecker's dining room that afternoon, Sal wondered how he could have failed to make even one sale. Hadn't he carried the bulky sample case from town to town? Hadn't he memorized all the square-foot prices for blue pearl and verde marina and the carrara marble? And even though the tombstone company kept sending him his leads, those neatly clipped notices—the obituaries of people in his territory—and he had kept reading them (he could never stop himself from reading them), he had never managed to make a single sale.

In his motel room that night after meeting Mr. Brecker, Sal stopped practicing scales for a moment and set his guitar on the edge of the bed. Except for the sound of new ice dropping into the coffers down the hall, the floor was quiet. He heard a light scuff of footsteps, then coins rolling into a slot and the soft thump of an aluminum can dropping to the bottom of the Coke machine.

Everything about this motel room was familiar—the same twenty-inch color television bolted to the dresser, the same odor of bare feet and cigarettes mixed in the carpet. The same acrylic paintings of sailboats hung on the wall. The boats moved smoothly across glistening water, some barely holding together against the force of a large and vicious storm that blew from somewhere outside the frame.

He sat on the edge of the bed, studying the swirling pattern in the well-worn bedspread. He remembered a recent newspaper article he'd read about scientists who had done a chemical analysis on motel room bedspreads and found sperm and tissue samples from hundreds of people. All those moments of ecstasy and remorse left behind like a geological record in the weave of the fabric.

Sal rose and dug his long fingers into the front pocket of his jeans. He fished out three quarters and went down the hallway to find the Coke machine. On the way back, he knocked on the doors of the two rooms where the rest of the band was staying. No answer. Just the sound of his knock echoing back. They were probably at the all-you-can-eat buffet.

Six months ago, he would have been with them at the Royal Fork, trying to see how many heaping platters of shrimp he could eat. Cupboard-was-bare hunger—once you experienced it, you never forgot. Even now that they were playing more, the band made so little money that when they came into the presence of food they lost all control. If they saw an all-you-can-eat sign on the side of the road, they took it as a challenge to their masculinity, like a notice for a skeet shooting contest or a big-man wrestle-off.

Six months ago, he would have been the one going back to the buffet for more chipped beef and macaroni salad. But afterward, back at the motel, he'd only feel stuffed and miserable. And all the buttered dinner rolls never held out the other hunger. Who knows how long it had been a part of him—an ache in his chest like a soft, unbroken wishbone.

Late at night, he felt it glow like phosphorus under his skin.

He remembered the board game he played with his sisters as a kid—Operation. These days, he felt like that surprised surgery patient with a red plastic nose who had numerous internal ailments that needed to be removed with a pair of delicate tweezers. But he didn't have butterflies in his stomach (in the shape of a butterfly), or water on the knee (in the shape of a bucket), or a wrenched ankle (in the shape of a monkey wrench), he had a hunger like a soft blue bone inside him.

Late at night after a gig, he'd think about last year and this year and next year, and he'd feel the hunger bone, floating foreign in his chest like a sponge left behind by a surgical team. Then he would wish for a pair of tongs, like those in Operation, or some other delicate instrument to clamp its icy prongs around the ache and lift it out. That's when he'd get out of bed and start to work on his songs. The empty feeling never went away completely, but writing the songs helped.

In front of his own door now, Sal dug in his back pocket for his room key. One of the perks of his sales job was that he got his own room, which the company paid for. It was good to have some privacy after all those years of four or five guys in a room, always someone's dirty socks and underwear on the floor.

From the outside, his life appeared to be improving. He had this second job now, which he could do on the road as they played. He was saving money for the recording project. He was writing songs. And the band was playing the circuit almost every week, thanks to their agent, Morrie, whose advice they had decided to stop ignoring.

The discussions with their agent always started with Morrie telling them how he'd been in the business for over thirty years. His office was dark and musty, with a flashing neon sign outside the window like something out of a private-eye movie. Then Morrie would bring his voice down and lean back in his squeaky chair. "Listen, boys," he would say, "to get along, you gotta go along."

Morrie was full of clichés like that. *Let sleeping dogs lie; to make money you gotta spend money.* His voice was deep and full of cigar smoke, as if he spent every waking moment talking on the phone. Morrie decided what bands worked, and bands only worked when they did what he wanted. Lately they'd decided to do what Morrie wanted.

Sal pulled back the motel room curtains and looked outside. The name of this place was New Vistas, but the view did not look new—just the same half-empty parking lot. It was that in-between time. All of last night's guests were checked out and on their way to some better place, and tonight's guests were still en route with the address of the New Vistas stuffed in their wallets. They were thinking about how they would jump into the pool, then fall into bed when they arrived.

From his second-floor window, Sal could see the buzzing neon sign flashing *Vacancy, Vacancy,* alternating with *Yes, Yes,* and the yellow lines of the empty parking lot, all in straight rows. The lot was waiting to fill up with cars, the rooms waiting to fill up with people, the vacancy sign waiting to be turned off for another night.

He wondered if rooms could take on a feeling. Sitting in Mr. Brecker's dining room that afternoon, Sal had sensed that the couple must have discussed the young wife's illness at that very table, their hands touching across the polished walnut surface. In the end, he wondered, had they dismantled the dining room table, removed its extensions to install a rented hospital bed?

That afternoon, all the photos and furniture had been back in place. But Sal felt that Mrs. Brecker must have reclined there in her last months, watching her children skip in and out to school, talking quietly with relatives who came for their last visits. It wasn't anything tangible, just a feeling. But each time Jack brought out another product sample and made a show of spit-polishing it with his white cloth, each time Jack said, *yes-sir* this and *yes-sir* that, Sal had the impulse to rise from his chair and excuse himself.

Something heavy had begun to ache in Sal's throat as he watched Mr. Brecker's wet eyes focus on the grainy whorls in the granite, forcing his index finger along the sample's deep patterns to keep himself from crying.

And Sal felt it again, something rising in him, when Jack Kelly stopped talking for a moment—because even *he* had to breathe sometimes—and there was a deathly quiet in the house. Only the ticking clock.

Just days before, this house would have been overrun with grieving relatives and neighbors coming over with warm casseroles. The history of the room buzzed under the surface, barely noticeable, like the quiet hum of cars passing by on the street outside the drawn curtains.

The obituary had said that Mrs. Brecker had died after a long illness, and Sal hadn't inquired further. All the dead people Sal knew had gone quickly—razor blades, car accidents, drugs.

Mr. Brecker had offered the details of his wife's long decline after the discovery of the brain tumor. The doctors hadn't even tried to operate. It felt eerie to sit in that room where death had so recently lingered, taking its time before finishing the job.

The Breckers' house was a three-bedroom rambler, ten or fifteen years old. The two daughters smiled through their braces from silver frames on the buffet. There was a modest fireplace in the living room, with a pair of matching beige love seats. Everything seemed to be in order that afternoon to Sal, but for one thing—what had become of Mrs. Brecker?

Perhaps Mr. Brecker had wondered this, too, because he raised his head and looked directly at Sal as if he had spoken. Sal sat back in his seat, blinking. He checked himself to see if he had spoken the words out loud, but, no, he had only thought them.

"Yes sir," Jack Kelly said then, picking up the Costa Rican carnelian as he noticed Mr. Brecker's new attentiveness. "We have to go deep into the rain forest for this stuff."

Mr. Brecker was in his mid-thirties and lived near a university. According to Jack's sales theory, chances were good that he was well read and interested in current issues such as the rain forest. This was number one of Jack Kelly's top-five rules of engagement—strive to find common ground.

"Uh-huh," Mr. Brecker said in a nasal tone. He appeared to be listening, but really, Sal could see, he wasn't. He was only responding in the places where Jack left pauses, just as Sal often had, saying things like "yes" and "I see" and "oh, really" when it appeared that Jack expected some verbal confirmation.

Mr. Brecker was deeply distracted—even Sal could see that. He'd sat at the table covering his face with his hands, his elbows propped heavily on the thick walnut table. If Sal were making the sales call alone, this is the point where he would have risen from the table and said, "Sir, I can see this is a difficult time for you," and then he would have packed up his samples and left, which is why, after six months, he'd yet to make a sale.

"Learn to swim," Jack Kelly had said, "or become fish food."

This is the story I'm saving for when I become famous, Sal said to himself over and over at Mr. Brecker's dining room table. Sometimes he told himself that his current life was only preparation for the future, and that the reason for paying attention now was so you could have some stories about the hard times later on. Even Morrie told him that: "Build up a rep, kid, some stories about your tough life before you made it in the bigs."

Good old Morrie. He figured people just ate up those stories about Sinatra living with cockroaches and Dylan starving and, you know, like Elvis buying a new car for everybody and his brother. So it was on Morrie's advice that Sal worked up a profile. He's a tequila drinker, Two Fingers, unless it's Dewars that's interviewing him for one of their celebrity profiles. In that case, he would become a scotch drinker.

Sal honed the profile, but no one came around to collect the stories; no one wanted to hear about what bars he drank in, which beds he slept in, which lonely window in the three-story tenement was his. No reporters were coming around to ask about the worst job he ever had before he made it.

Was it so bad to be an unknown songwriter with a bunch of unrecorded songs, and music that played only in your head? With the money he was going to make pushing rock, he planned to go into the studio and record a CD—something solid to show for his efforts. But Mr. Brecker had shown him again that day how impossible it was to close a sale.

"You know, we have an excellent payment plan," Jack Kelly had said, trying to move Mr. Brecker toward a commitment. Sal had looked up from the whorls in the dining room table to see Mr. Brecker hedging. He could read the signs not so much on Mr. Brecker, but on Jack Kelly who had developed a thin layer of sweat on his forehead.

Finally Mr. Brecker came clean. He had better wait until the spring, he said, until the ground settled. "Nothing seems possible right now," he finally whispered.

"Oh, yes, certainly," Jack Kelly waved his hand in a free-trial-no-obligation way.

"I'm sorry about wasting your time," Mr. Brecker apologized, fumbling with his large empty hands, so clean and tender they looked like they'd been dipped in bleach.

"No waste," Jack said, pursing his lips tight and beginning to clear the table.

It pained Sal to see the slow, methodical way that Jack folded each sample into a swatch of white cloth, as if he were packing away bars of gold. He left the Pyrenees star blue out the longest. It was his personal favorite and the most expensive in the line. He wanted to give Mr. Brecker the extra moment to see the merchandise, to see the solidity of the granite and marble, so that he would feel its absence somewhere in his bones after it disappeared from before his eyes.

"It's just so hard," Mr. Brecker said, a small crack opening in his voice. "We didn't prepare."

"No problem." Jack said, dismissing him with his hand. "Understand perfectly."

And now that Mr. Brecker had found words and the story of his wife's death began to tumble from him, Jack seemed to fold up the samples more quickly and return them to his case. Sal had sat through dozens of these stories. In the last few months he'd heard about accidents and aneurysms and long bouts with cancer. He'd heard about loved ones who were there one second and gone the next. He'd heard the snap of the finger that went with the story. Sal had listened through them all, sometimes turning his own face to keep from crying.

"There, there," Jack Kelly said, tapping his palm on the table, as if to awaken Mr. Brecker out of the sleep of his grief. Jack was wearing a heavy gold ring with a chunk of diamond in it. The knock of the gold on Mr. Brecker's dining room table sounded like a gavel calling a courtroom to order.

Jack Kelly's number two rule of engagement: Don't allow the bereaved to dwell on the *how* of death. "Talk about an hour eater," Jack said.

Mr. Brecker rose from his chair. He went to the closet to get their coats. "Sorry to go on and on," he apologized. "I just forget sometimes and think that everyone knew her," he said, talking to them from inside his hall closet. He returned with the shrunken skins of their raincoats hanging in his hands. "You really oughta known her."

In the foyer where they said their uncomfortable goodbyes, Sal saw himself reflected in the hallway mirror. It was an old-fashioned washstand with a porcelain bowl and a large stand-up mirror. When he saw his eyes, red and bugged out from lack of sleep, he felt even more ashamed. It was one of those unexpected moments when you catch a glimpse of yourself in a public bathroom or a store window, and you think, "Hey, that's me, out in the world." And at that moment, you either like what you see or you don't.

Back at the New Vistas, Sal studied his face again in the bathroom mirror as he dried his hair, waiting for the double knock on the door that said it was time to go and play. And as he traced the lines in his skin in the bright bathroom light, he found he still did not like what he saw.

Know your markets. This is the third rule of engagement that both Jack Kelly and Morrie had tried for months to teach him. No matter how personally meaningful the song you are playing is to you, if people don't know it, they won't dance to it.

"Nobody wants to get stuck out on the dance floor," Morrie complained over the phone, "trying to dance to one of those 7/8 parts you like to stick into the middle of songs." Every week Morrie had a new complaint about Sal's music—nobody wants to look like they got caught in a strobe light, nobody wants to hear about how eating red meat is a reason to have the blues. It was a shame, Sal thought. He knew they were good songs.

At one time the band had played only their own music. They had a conviction that playing other people's music would rot you slowly from the inside out. But that was before the winter, before they were starving and the power company was threatening to shut off the heat. Finally, one day, Morrie called up. He said he was on their side, and he understood their dilemma, but there was just no sustaining market in this area for original music.

"People want to hear what's on the radio," he told Sal.

"Morrie," Sal said, "somebody had to *write* the stuff that's on the radio." But Morrie considered this a fine point of distinction. When he called, he just said, I got work for you, or I don't. So November was lean, which is when Morrie called to say, "Shed your pride for once, Sal. I got a hot gig for you. Big bucks, just sixty miles away."

He assured the band that they would be playing for people they would never see again. They could play under an assumed name, the Rabid Dogs or the Petting Monkeys. "Take the money at the end of the night and run." They all agreed; it would be a caper.

It had turned out to be some sort of dance club—yuppie businessmen and their wives. The band that was booked to play canceled at the last minute, and the dance club members were pissing in their pants with joy just to see any band walk through the door with their gear.

The band had to play fifties music, which they faked through. It was just *one-four-five, one-four-five,* the same chords all night, and most of the lyrics Sal just made up as he went along. He didn't worry much about the words, because he figured anyone who might have known the original lyrics back in the glorious fifties was probably too interested in the stock market to comment on a missing phrase here and there.

In the end, it turned out okay for everyone. These folks

were eating it up, sweating through the armpits of their sports coats, doing those twirl-my-baby-over-my-back moves all night long. At the end of the night the band got paid just fine, no problems. As soon as they finished, they got busy packing when up stepped this dude with a cigar who asked Sal, "Can I speak to you in private?" This was when they went off to a corner and the man offered him the tombstone job.

"We got something in common, kid," the man with the cigar said.

"Oh, really, sir?" Sal said, his hands politely at his sides, as if he were talking to a high school principal.

"You deal in rock," the man leaned forward, a little drunk, pointing the tip of his cigar at Sal, "and I deal in rock." Then he let out a raucous laugh, the phlegm letting loose in his chest. "You got charisma, kid," he said, pointing to Sal, "and you don't even know it." Then the man reached into his pocket for a business card: Lakes Granite & Monument.

Sal looked down, fingering the card. "Nah," he said, "I'm a musician." He wasn't right for the job, he tried to explain. Musicians weren't dependable. They traveled from place to place.

"That's the beauty of selling tombstones," the man said, licking the tip of his cigar. "We got dead people wherever you go." All Sal had to do was advise the front office which part of the circuit he'd be traveling from month to month, and they would forward the leads for that territory to him.

You know how they say you should never go grocery shopping when you're hungry? Sal discovered that you should never take a job when you're hungry. Not like the kind of hunger he felt deep in his bones that night. On the way home it all began to seem reasonable to him. He could save every penny he made, live on saltines and peanut butter, and put all the money in a savings account. Then he could afford to record all his songs. He could almost feel it in his hands—the heaviness of the CD he would make.

The next morning, Jack Kelly had appeared at his front door for the first time with all his sales materials: a briefcase full of granite and marble samples, and a manila envelope stuffed full of newspaper clippings, obituaries for the most recently departed in his sales territory.

Jack Kelly, as he found out later, was Lakes Granite & Monument's number one salesman. Jack's greatest claim to fame was that several years before he had happened upon a mad widow, so crazed in her grief that he had convinced her to buy a mausoleum with a carrara marble carapace.

"Forty thousand big ones," Jack had whooped at the kitchen table that first morning, telling Sal the whole mausoleum story start to finish, a story Sal would hear many more times. They were each having a cup of instant coffee that Sal had scrounged out of the empty cupboard. Sal's head was throbbing from the night before—all that fifties music—and all he really wanted to do was go back to sleep, but Jack kept talking.

Never trust the undertaker, Jack Kelly said to Sal on that first morning. Never trust his package deals—the candle-lit vigils with the organ music playing softly in the background, the gold-plated coffins, the promise of shady plots and hand-carved tombstones—all those painful details the bereaved would rather avoid dealing with.

"It's all arranged," the undertaker will say. And he might

be wringing his hands with grief in the front room, but in the back room he's rubbing those thin, dry palms together over the two hundred percent markup he's applied to all the paraphernalia of death. The way Jack explained it to Sal, they were doing the people a favor by offering them a superior product at a fair price.

Mrs. Brecker's obituary—what Sal would have done with it had he seen it first. He did not see it first; Jack Kelly brought it with him from the front office. If Sal had seen it first, he would have filed it in the *tragic* pile.

It was a triage he'd devised to organize his leads from the front office. First he liked to give them all a fair read through before he separated them into piles. After that he spread them out on the bedspread from right to left. In the middle he had the *tragic* pile, which was for people like Mrs. Brecker, people who had gone too quickly, people in their middle years who had kids and spouses.

On the right-hand side, he placed the obituaries he judged *sad but expected*. These were people in their eighties and nineties. Sal realized this was harsh categorization, but there was never enough information in these obituaries to make an informed decision.

On the left he had a pile for the *unfathomables*. These were the infants, the kids dead in their teens. It broke his heart to find one of these, and he could never bear to make a call on the families. On the top of each clipping, a date had been written in, noting when the obituary had appeared in the paper. By law, salesmen were required to wait ten days before soliciting the family. "A grace period," Jack Kelly said, "and then they're fair game.

The morning after the call to Mr. Brecker's house, Sal was reading through the obituaries, noting the names of the spouses left behind, whole lives and careers summarized down to three paragraphs, when Jack Kelly appeared at his motel room door.

"You still here?" Sal said as he swung open the door.

"I gotta look after you, kid," Jack said, hulking into the small opening. "I'm givin' you one last chance." He sat down on the edge of the bed and began looking through the carefully organized piles.

"Sometimes it's hard to get a feel for these," he said, his large hands moving over the obituaries as if they were a ouija board. Sal moved a little closer, placing his body between Jack and the notices.

"What's this?" Jack asked, holding up a clipping. It was nearly a foot long and folded several times, the tail unfurling as Jack lifted it in the air to read.

"See, here," he said. "This man owned a photography studio for fifty-two years."

Mr. Colesio, Sal thought, he's got Mr. Colesio. Sal jumped at Jack Kelly, trying to grab the clipping.

"This is a good granite lead," Jack said, stepping away. "Comes from a large Italian family." There was wonder in his voice. "Thirteen kids," he said, almost giddy. Jack's number four rule of engagement: choose a subject with lots of heirs.

"Thirty-five grandkids," Sal groaned, feeling a little sick.

Mrs. Colesio, when she answers the door, is ready for them. She's wearing the traditional mourning garb: black skirt, black blouse, black sweater, black shawl draped across her shoulders. Fortunately, it's a color that looks good on her, because she's likely to wear it for the rest of her earthly days.

She escorts the two men to a dim parlor, where she seats them in chairs worn thin. The parlor is so small that their knees almost touch as they sit.

"So sorry to hear about Mr. Colesio's passing," Jack Kelly says quietly, straining for breath as he sits down. "A pillar of the community," he adds.

Mrs. Colesio nods silently. Her hair is gathered in a bun, the gray knot coming together at the back of her neck. In her hands, she holds a rosary. The beads are black and no longer shiny. They are worn down from years of constant touching. Mrs. Colesio works the rosary as Jack Kelly speaks to her. She pauses for several moments on one bead and then, that round of prayers completed, moves her old fingers to find the next bead.

All the while Jack Kelly unpacks the samples, she works the rosary. Jack Kelly perches his large body uncomfortably in the tiny chair, balancing the samples on a white towel spread over his briefcase. She works the rosary as Jack Kelly speaks to her about the art of stone cutting, about engraving, about honoring the dead.

Then he takes out the verde marina, the one from southern India that is so rare, and Mrs. Colesio sets down the beads and picks up the heavy green rock. She looks at it for a long time, rubbing her thumbs in small circles, considering its weight, its color, the dark concentric circles that swirl within it.

The room takes on a full silence, the old furniture listens. "How much of this can you get for me?" she finally asks in a heavy accent.

At this question, Jack Kelly's back stiffens. From where Sal sits, he can hear the cash register chinging in Jack's head, his eyeballs rolling in their sockets—everything coming up dollar signs. A thin layer of sweat develops on Jack Kelly's upper lip, as he contemplates his best answer.

From his training, Sal knows that this is Jack Kelly's number five rule of engagement: know how much to pitch, at the right price. When will less per square foot yield you a larger order, which results in more profit overall?

Jack Kelly twists in his seat, considering. Mrs. Colesio sits with the verde marina in her hands, drawing circles with her thumbs.

In the silence, Sal becomes aware of a heaviness in his limbs and a throbbing in his chest. He feels himself sinking into the soft cushions of the old chair. The back of his neck is hot, and he feels lightheaded, a little sick to his stomach.

As Jack Kelly draws a breath to speak, Sal looks around the room and down the hallway. Can he make it to the bathroom? What he needs now is the feel of cool porcelain against his forehead. But if he interrupts and asks permission, Jack will kill him.

Then he remembers an article he read about paramedics who observed that a high percentage of people die in bathrooms—probably because that's where you go when you feel awful. Had Mr. Colesio died in the bathroom?

A feeling of panic rises in Sal's stomach, and his legs lift him involuntarily from the chair. Jack Kelly lets out a little huffing sound, and Mrs. Colesio looks up at Sal with moist eyes, a look of profound understanding on her face.

Sal leans over and takes her hands. The heaviness of the stone rises between them. "So nice to have met you," he says and cups her hands in his own. Her face is beatific, as if a soft blue light shines from under her skin.

Sal moves through the old sitting room quickly and closes the front door behind him. Outside, he sets off running. His heart feels good beating hard in his chest.

When he gets to the New Vistas, he runs up the stairs to his room, taking two steps at a time. He finds his guitar resting in its black case in the corner. He undoes the latches and runs his hand over the shiny strings. The mahogany body feels smooth beneath his fingertips.

He pulls the instrument to his chest and begins to play—old songs he had forgotten, new songs he'd never thought of before. Everything sounds good to him at this moment. The Lakes Granite & Monument sample case rests heavy in the corner. He will take it to the front desk for Jack to pick up later.

The sun shines bright in the room, a lightness overtaking Sal as he practices. Soon the guys will come knocking to tell him it's time to go play. I am history, Sal thinks, as his hands move across the neck, reeling out an unbroken string of notes. *History, history, history.* And with each new note he plays, it becomes more of a certainty.

WAITING FOR DEAN

His friends didn't like to see him thirsty. They sent little messages of encouragement to the stage, small notes like "Party down, Dean" and "Kick ass, man," sprawled on napkins along with the golden shots the smiling waitresses delivered to Dean. The shimmering glasses of Quervo, Jack Daniels, Southern Comfort collected at his feet, varying in shades from pale yellow to orange to dark molasses brown.

Soon the empty and full shot glasses surrounded the drum set, some tipped over, emptied of their contents, some lapping at his feet like hungry tongues of yellow, ready to burn down his throat in the next thirsty moment, as Dean stomped and sliced away at the high hat. Kicking the bass drum with the bottom of his boot, he took time to pop his gum, twirl his drumsticks, and wink at the prettiest dancers.

Everybody wanted Dean. Women blushed, drunks leaned in, bikers threw off their leather and kicked back in their chairs. Perhaps it was the bond of drink, but Dean was naturally sociable. When he stepped offstage, they swallowed him in a hungry circle. He dove into their masses, slapping every back and shaking hands, talking big and friendly as a used car salesman.

The band often found themselves waiting on stage with the lights low at the end of a break, hands running up and down the necks of their guitars, scanning the crowd for Dean. Under the dim swinging light behind the bar, the manager drew endless taps, poured tequila poppers. His three-day beard, the dark circles under his eyes calculating the amount of pay he would deduct at the end of the week.

They waited like this so often, they decided to change their name to Waiting for Dean, which only brought more fans of Dean to the club. Next to him, the rest of the band was like the ugly sisters at the end of the fairy tale, sweeping the floor with their guitars and weeping alone late into the night.

But sometimes mercy was shown and a round of flaming shots appeared for the band, carried by the waitress on a tray over her head. Then the band stopped playing and called for a toast, a roar going up in the crowd as people raised beer bottles and wine glasses, short glasses and snifters, and the band lifted their burning shots, blowing out the flames and tossing back their heads, the hot liquid warming the deep rivulets of their bodies.

These were the days of too many friends, when everybody waited for Dean—the longest wait coming at the end of the night when the final chord was struck and the crowd rose to their feet shouting *Encore, encore.*

It was then that Dean hopped from his stool and jumped off the edge of the stage, saying he had to drain his parrot, take a whiz, swim the Danube, see a man about a horse—he had a million ways to say he had to take a piss—and the crowd waited on the dance floor, and the band waited on stage with their hands on their instruments. All of them chanting wildly for Dean, Dean, Dean, in the bathroom, pissing a golden arc of sunlight into the swirling porcelain bowl.

Going to California

I was between sets when I ran into Jed, my old guitar player. He was one of those well-preserved hippies from the older generation of musicians I played with when I first came to this town. Most of them were fried to a crispy brown from hash and pickled pink by bourbon in their twenties, then saved by good women and AA in their thirties. It was Jed who told me about what happened to Sam.

Most of these older guys had crossed over to country or migrated to Holiday Inn bands. They traded in their blue jeans for Dockers, their ponytails for short layer cuts, and their Flying Vs for Fender Strats. But even now, Jed still wore wire rims and long straight hair parted down the middle. I liked that about him. Even though he'd managed to quit drinking, he still insisted on saying *man* at least once in every sentence.

"You're looking good, man," he said to me, even though I was a woman, or a chick, as he used to call me back when we played together—the chick singer—which is what we all used to call ourselves back then, before any of us knew better. Then he told me about Sam.

"Sorry to lay all this on you," he said, flipping his hair out from under his collar. He slid a cigarette out of my pack on the bar and lit it. The break music was pumping loud and the crowd was on their feet, milling. It was hard to hear. Jed leaned into me, yelled in my ear. "It happened months ago, man. I figured for sure you knew."

All the rest of the night as we played, I thought of Sam finally reaching that place he'd been grasping at for years. When they found him, Jed told me, he'd been dead for hours. I tried to picture Sam's hands stretched out in a silhouette on some motel room sheets, and then I thought about his fingers splayed wide on his keyboard, the way I remembered them, playing some diminished chord nobody else in the band could reproduce or comprehend.

He always played hunched over with a cigarette dangling between his lips. Even then, when he was half drunk, he had some mysterious effect on women. Later, when I started to play with him, I saw from on stage how his hands had their own kind of life in music, his fingers easing into a chord, angling on and off the black and white keys, rolling through the variations. Standing by him, you hoped he might accidentally brush his hands against you or circle themselves around your waist.

That night when I got home, I found my bottle of Quervo and sat at the kitchen table thinking about those hands inside the cufflinks of some dark suit buried in a hole on the south side. And when I thought of that, I poured myself a shot and then another and then another. "Goddamn you," I said each time, and lifted the shot glass to my lips. "Goddamn you fucking son of a bitch."

Jed told me that Sam's wife was selling his equipment to pay off the funeral expenses. The next afternoon when I got to the club for rehearsal, I found the matchbook where Jed had written the number, and I picked up the phone.

I don't know why I called her. The woman had nothing to do with me. She was just his young widow. I had known Sam back when he was unhappily married to his first wife.

"I'm interested in the keyboard you're selling," I said when she picked up. I was calling from the pay phone at the club, and I hoped she wasn't hearing the crack of cue balls in the background.

"Oh, yes," she said, seeming to understand perfectly. I checked her voice for a sign of discomfort with the subject, some catch of the breath. I heard nothing. In the background, there was a lot of chatter, women talking about permanents and fingernails and men. I had called her at work. She owned Josie's, a hair salon she had named after herself.

"Could you come by my house after six?" she asked.

"Sure," I said quickly, before I had a chance to think about it. I wanted to see how he had done in the part of his life that came after me.

Josie's house was in a new neighborhood on the south side of town, on one of those streets that doesn't go straight through to anywhere. And if you got on the wrong street, you ran the risk of never being heard from again.

This is how people came to settle in these neighborhoods, I thought. You take a wrong turn one day and try your best to get back on the main road, but you only get more and more lost. Eventually the bank sends out a service van, gives you an E-Z term financing loan, and you move in the very next day.

I found the house easily enough with the directions Josie had given me. I walked up the long driveway, past the flower beds and green, trimmed lawn. It was a great house, really, and I tried to imagine Sam there, lounging on the front lawn in his black turtleneck and Ray-Bans, with a vodka gimlet in a short glass balancing on his stomach. I rang the doorbell, and she answered right away.

"Come on in," she said. "Glad you could come." Right away, I saw how nice she was, not just one of those people who tries to be nice but really isn't. She was small and perky — genuine, I guess — and looking around I could see how lovely the house was, with the sun coming through circular windows in wide, unbroken swaths. And there was tan carpet on the floor, and watercolor art on the walls. It was quiet, too. I tried to imagine Sam's tall, noisy body in this house.

She was twenty-eight years old and a widow. I tried to imagine that. But she seemed light and easy, like one of those people who just pops out of bed happy in the morning. What had she done with her time, I wondered, while Sam slept late into the afternoon, his body sprawled over the edges of the bed.

A woman like her would want to take long walks around the neighborhood at sundown, admiring other people's flower beds, but Sam hated the outdoors. He had a nasty hack and dark circles ringing his eyes. "Honey, there's too much fresh air in the world," he would say to me, as he lit a new cigarette with the burning tip of his old one. I guess the seventies were the decade when we didn't believe we were going to live past thirty. So we didn't worry about how we were going to look at middle age.

"Would you like something to drink?" Josie asked, leading me through the house. And I knew she meant coffee or tea.

"No thanks," I said, thinking how smart Sam was to find someone who was independent. No matter what happened to him, he knew she would carry on alone, because that's what the partner of a musician has to do.

We turned the corner, and she opened the door into a cool room with the curtains drawn at the back of the house. Inside, keyboards were set up on metal stands; metronomes and sheet music were scattered around on shelves. A Fender Rhodes sat in the middle of the room, as if its owner had just run out to the store for a pack of Marlboros.

Although it was in a completely different house, in another neighborhood in another decade, this room looked exactly like the room where Sam and I used to practice when I first joined his band. It was his job to teach me all the songs before we went to full rehearsal. He and I spent hours huddled over this electric piano, his fingers in a relaxed pyramid on the keys, pounding out another tune.

"I haven't had a chance to clean up in here," Josie apologized.

"That's okay," I said, running my hand over the smooth top of the Rhodes. My fingers left thin trails in the dust.

"I'm looking to part with all of this stuff," Josie said,

pointing around the room. She reminded me of one of those TV spokesmodels, her thin hand floating lightly through the air as though she were demonstrating what was behind curtain number three.

I sat down at the electric piano, ran my fingers along the keys. Without the current, it gave off little bell tones, just enough to hear the notes and the sound of the hammers hitting the metal tines.

"That was my husband's favorite instrument," she said, twisting her lips into a sad smile.

"Your husband?"

"He was a local performer," she said. "Perhaps you've seen him." She pointed to all the band promotion shots on the wall, mostly black-and-white, eight-by-ten glossies. You could trace the evolution of haircuts and fashion—from bell-bottoms to boot-cuts—and the groupings of men, usually five or six, with the band name sprawled above the booking agency's logo. Since high school, Sam had been in maybe fifteen bands. As I moved down the line, the faces got older and bearded, the eyes more deep-set. And I noticed that the photo from our band was not among them.

"No, I don't think so," I said. "I don't know a lot of musicians." I sat back down behind the piano and ran my fingers through a progression of chords.

"It's nice to hear music in this room again," she said. "I'd forgotten how good it sounds." She straightened some stacks of sheet music on the shelf. "Do you play professionally?" she asked.

"I just tinker," I said. "Mostly I'm a singer."

"Sam loved working with singers," she said, leaning against a bookshelf. "Said he liked the feel of a human voice running up and down his spine." She looked at the floor then and laughed, as if she were trying to force something down inside her.

"This piano feels great," I said, thinking about how Sam always wanted to go to California, just pack up and head to L.A. These keys were the last thing he touched that night in Florida, and I wondered what was the last song he played, what song could play itself backwards off the keys.

"I think I'll take this one," I finally said.

"Good," she said quickly. She seemed glad to have something settled. "There's a road case that goes with it," she added, moving across the room toward the door. "I'll get it for you."

While she was gone, I started tearing down the keyboard. I managed to set it on its side and unscrew the braces and the legs. I unhooked the cords and wrapped them in a tight coil on the floor beside the speaker. Josie returned with the hardshell cover, and we hooked the top to the hinges on the case.

While I wrote out my check, I noticed she stayed bent over the keyboard, running her fingers across its keys one last time, then she closed the lid and snapped the latches shut.

We managed to get the Rhodes through the house without scraping the woodwork. We leaned over the heavy bulk of the keyboard, bent our knees and loaded it into my trunk. The back of my car dipped low with the weight.

It felt good to be out in the sun again. In the distance, I could hear kids playing, the hard *thunk* of someone kicking a ball. "Thanks so much," I said, handing her the check. I stood at the back of the car with my hand resting on the trunk.

"No," she said, modestly, "thank *you*." She folded the check and placed it in her left front shirt pocket, then she pulled a small wad of papers from her other shirt pocket. On the top was a photo of Sam, sitting behind his Rhodes with an icy drink sweating in his right hand. He was looking at the camera in the natural way he had during his best moments—that dark, bearded smile ready to erupt into a laugh that could be heard from anywhere in the club. Even in the dim photo, the deep articulation of veins on his hands from so many hours of playing showed through.

"These are the kind of hands," I said, "that you're lucky to be born with." She nodded beside me. I turned to go.

"He would want you to have this," she said, forcing the photograph into my hand. We walked along the side of the car. "Play the piano in good health," she said as I opened my front door.

I bent to get in behind the wheel. She stood in the driveway and waved good-bye, as I put the car in reverse. My muffler put down a hard scrape on her driveway.

At the stop, I watched the kids jump rope and hopscotch in their driveways. Behind the lace curtains, mothers and fathers were reading papers and fixing dinner.

When I shifted into gear, the engine gunned and my car burned a loud blast through the quiet street. The kids stopped in their play and looked in my direction.

I felt the weight of the piano shift in my trunk as I turned each corner. Going backward through Josie's directions, I found my way to the main road. Rush hour traffic had backed up the boulevard, everybody trying to get home for dinner. I sat in the intersection for a long time, with my blinker going. Then I took a sharp left into the sun at the first opening.

BIG GUITAR SOUND

Although everyone told Randy he'd have to go to Spain to get the truly big guitar sound, the kind that comes barreling out of the guitar like the bulls out of the gates at Pamplona, he thought he'd try Des Moines first, a place called Last Chance Guitars, famous for having refused Dylan use of the bathroom one time back in the eighties during his Jesus phase when he really had to go, but the clerk didn't recognize the pout behind the sunglasses that curved, dark and mirrored, around his famous face.

Everything about Randy was oversized—massive hambone hands, long strike-a-pose legs, big hair threatening to topple him as he bent to play a lick, his tongue out, dreaming of finding a sound as thick as cream off a spout. At the Last Chance he found the metal zone, a row of pedals, strung together, LEDs popping on and off like Christmas lights.

He tried the flanger that doubled his tone, made him two instead of one, still sounding less than a trip to Spain.

He tried the baby tremolo, pulsating through the neck of his guitar. He shook the life from it, stomping on the chorus, a thick, shimmering sound rising, the wah-wah, the super fuzz, the hyper-turbo-overdrive-grunge-phase shifter that made him sound like thirteen chain saws gnawing through plywood—half a continent away from Memphis and still not as big as if he'd gone to Spain.

Big Doings at the Pavilion

A little over halfway to the gig, the bass player sat up in the back of the rocking van and looked around in surprise. They called him Mean One, not because he was mean, but because he appeared mean with his rough face and thick scruffy beard. "Ah, no," Mean One said. His arms fell limp at his sides.

"Ah, shit," he said, "ah, motherfuck." No one heard this, not the guitar players sprawled in sleep on the van floor around him, not even the driver up front, who chewed gum and watched the road with an unblinking stare.

"Hey," Mean One yelled at the driver. "Hey, Boner." It was a nickname the band gave the driver one night back in Gillette. There was a story that went along with the name about a woman with long brown hair, but the driver didn't acknowledge either of them anymore—not the woman or the name. The rest of the band slept or pretended to sleep, their ears numbed by the truck's constant rattle of rivets, the squeak and groan of equipment shifting in the back, and the roar of the tires meeting asphalt.

Mean One moved through the van in a half-crouch, spreading his hands wide to keep his balance in the lurching vehicle. He waved his arms at the driver in the rearview mirror. Boner was wearing headphones as he drove, blasting out the loudest metal he could find. The rest of the band moved their long legs out of the way. They were whiskered and bad-breathed, a little burned out from the night before, and thinking about the long night ahead.

"Hey," Mean One finally reached the front of the van, weaving and balancing himself between the front seats. He lifted a headphone off of Boner's ear. From the tiny speaker a miniature heavy metal band leaked out—small angry screams, the razor static of amped-up guitars, snare drums, and tom-toms cutting through the tiny breaks.

"Did you pack my bass?" Mean One yelled, his body swaying to the movement of the truck.

"What?" Boner asked, as if coming out of a deep sleep. He pulled the headphones off, letting them rest around his neck, the heavy metal band beating small music on his chest.

"My bass," Mean One said, moving his arms as if playing guitar. "Did you pack my bass?" And at this, everyone in the truck groaned.

This is the way it always happened. They might be playing poker on the way to a one-nighter, and just as he discards an eight of hearts, he'll say, "Did I pack my bass?" He'll say it in that worried tone. "I'm pretty sure it's not back there." He'll repeat it over and over as they roar down the highway, covering one mile and then another, until pretty soon they can all see his guitar case not in the back of the van where it should be, but leaning against the bricks of his bookcase at his girlfriend's apartment. Then they will pull the truck over to the shoulder, get out, and open up the van.

Microphone stands and cymbal cases rain down on them when they crack open the back door. "Goddamn it," Boner will say. He has defied physical laws to get everything packed in.

Of course it's always there, long and cool and slim in its black case, packed in a row with the other guitars. But nobody would have rested until they knew for sure. It was the number one obsessive thing that every guitar player had nightmares about—forgetting your axe—and so if there was any question at all you had to check it and check again, just like you had to check your fly when you came out of the bathroom, running your fingers along the top of the zipper, just to make sure it was really shut.

That's why they called him Mean One. Because he looked mean when he hammered out the notes on his bass—not with a pick or his fingers, but with his righteous fist.

They also called him Mean One because they were convinced he was a bit of a sadist, and that all along he knew his bass *was* there. And that's why no one believed him that day on their way to the Bourbon County Fair in Kansas, when he perked up with that worried look.

"Oh, shut up," everyone groaned, trying to go back to sleep.

But when he finally convinced them to stop fifty miles later, it really was not there. His black Warlock B.C. Rich bass with the beautiful twenty-four-fret rosewood fingerboard and the three-way switch that allowed him a variety of tones, everything from chain saws to chocolate pudding with the flip of a switch.

It was not there—not the stainless steel flat round strings, or the well-made alder body, with the points and angles, and the cut-out bottom that reminded you, when you saw it, of a woman's crotch. The bass that purred like a nasty girl when you ran your hands along its sharp curves. It simply was not there.

They stood for a while on the shoulder of the road. Kansas spread wide around them, the rolling green and tan of wheat fields and grassy pastures, the long yawn of Highway 69. A cold breeze blew at their backs and swirled their long hair into their faces. They huddled together and pulled their collars around their necks. Cars whizzed by, never slowing to stop. The band stood with their hands in their pockets as one after another took turns looking inside the truck for the long black Warlock case.

Boner stepped away from the truck. "How big is this town we're going to?" His duties included driving the van, setting up the equipment, and running sound. The band would never have made it anywhere without him.

"About five thousand people," someone said.

"Do you think they have a music store?" Mean One asked, but really he was way ahead of them. He was thinking, It's already four-thirty and even if there is a music store where they're going, it won't be open by the time they get there.

An hour later when they reached Pleasanton, they found a phone booth outside a faded Skelly station with sand-beaten pumps and a Coke machine that still dispensed bottles.

They checked the yellow pages, surprised to find a listing for a music store—Mom & Pop's. It took fifteen rings, but someone answered the phone when Mean One dialed the number.

The voice on the other end of the line sounded breathless, like he'd climbed stairs to reach the phone. "Did I catch you leaving?" Mean One asked, trying to sound anxious, like he didn't want to put anyone out. When preparing to ask a favor, he knew, a little small talk at the top of the conversation goes a long way.

"Heavens no," the voice wheezed. It was an ancient voice, old as Ben Franklin.

"By God," Mean One covered the receiver and hissed at Boner, "I think I've got Pops himself."

"Well, sir," Mean One said into the receiver, "I'm with the orchestra that's performing out at the county fair this evening." He was careful to avoid the words *band* and *gig* because he suspected these words would scare Pops off. It would be like coming in with two loaded shotguns hoisted on your shoulders and saying, *Yeah, we're the band. Give us your equipment.*

"Oh, heavens," Pops gushed into the phone. "What can I do you boys for?"

Pops was an old jazz musician, as it turned out. "Quit playing in forty-six and never looked back," he told Mean One when he dropped off the bass. He was so thrilled to be called into service that he delivered the instrument to the dance hall at the fairgrounds.

By now the band had most of the equipment unloaded,

and the hall was busy with the activity of setting up, everyone going about their business—wiring P.A. columns, hanging lights.

"Yep," Pops said, "big doings at the pavilion." His face beamed as he looked around the dance floor, holding a guitar case in his hand. "I blew a few notes in this joint."

All around, heavy black boxes overflowed with speaker cables, guitar amps, lighting fixtures. The guitar players were tuning their guitars, the drummer was stomping on his kick drum.

"Of course, that was in the forties," Pop said, turning to Mean One, who stood beside him now, afraid to see what kind of a bass Pop had brought.

"I was a horn man myself," the old man said, a touch of sadness in his voice. "Of course, everything's different now."

"I'll bet," says Mean One. In a way, he would have liked the conversation to go on forever—to hear Pop talk about the big-band glory days, and what greats played this stage, to hear what year they passed through, and what songs they played. Mean One would have preferred to continue this conversation rather than see what was in the dusty black case that Pop held in his left hand.

"I think this will do you just fine," Pops said finally, and limped across the dance floor to the nearest table. He swung the black case flat and snapped open the latches. When he pulled open the cover, a candy-apple red bass appeared. It was a hollow-body, deep as a cereal box with two S-shaped sound holes, one on either side of the wide body.

Mean One swallowed hard. He pulled the guitar from the case. It was light to the touch, as if made from cardboard. It felt like it might crumble in his hands.

"Had this in the store for a long time," Pop said, blowing a cloud of dust from the head of the guitar. "Don't even know if it's in tune."

Mean One got out his black leather guitar strap, the one with the viper fangs hissing up and down its length. Somehow the strap had made it to the gig while the guitar had not. Mean One hooked one end to the peg on the bottom of the guitar and swung the strap over his neck. He fastened the strap to the peg on top of the guitar, and felt the bass settle into his hands.

"If you fall in love with this one," Pops called behind him as he walked out the door, "I'd be willing to give you boys a hell of a deal."

It was a toy guitar, really, the kind you saw in the Sears catalog when you were ten and you begged your mom to order it, and then when it came you sat on your bed for hours and studied the E-Z-2-Play lessons in the Mel Bay book *(this is a how to hold a guitar, this is how to hold a pick),* until you got bored and put it back in the case and let it gather dust under your bed. Then your mom had a garage sale and palmed it off on someone else.

Mean One stepped on stage, the guitar hanging lightly on the strap. It seemed to float weightless in front of him, a full ten pounds lighter than his Warlock. "Let's see how it sounds," he said, plugging it into the bass amp and turning the volume up to nine. He swirled around and swatted the strings with his oversized paw. Out came a sound like two rubber bands twanging against an aluminum can. Everybody stopped what they were doing and laughed.

"That's not so bad," Boner said, taking off his headphones and coming out from behind the soundboard. But, oh, it was bad.

"Yeah," one of the guitar players added, stepping to the middle of the dance floor and putting his hand to his chin like he was listening through the P.A. to get the total effect. "It sounds kind of cool out here."

"Yeah, right," Mean One said, banging out the opening riff for "Smoke on the Water." It sounded like a diesel engine chugging in the middle of winter with the wrong mixture of fuel. This made everyone bend over with laughter.

"We can fix it," Boner said, opening the case that held all the guitar-whiz-kid gizmos. He picked out a distortion box, a wah-wah pedal, an EQ, and a compressor. "Here," he said, thrusting them at Mean One. "This stuff can even make a twin prop sound like a guitar."

"Yeah, right," Mean One said, pawing the guitar again, rapping out the bass line for "Cocaine." It sounded like a duck call blown through an amplifier. This got the attention of the bartender. He was busy stocking the Miller Lite cooler, but he looked up from his rows of beer cases and began to laugh.

"Big doings at the Pavilion," Boner said, and pushed up the slider for the bass guitar channel. The bass sound rose like an amorphous gray fog in the room. The waitress swabbing the tables and the doorman sweeping the floor stopped their work and began to laugh.

But Mean One wasn't listening anymore, not to the tone of his guitar, not to the laughter in the distance. He stood on stage, hulking and menacing in his black leather, and beat his hands on the strings that barely held to the neck of the candy-apple red guitar. Soon the dancers would come and throw their bodies into the music.

He held his small piece of stage that night in tight pants and spiked wristbands, looking especially mean, beating the sounds out of this cherry-red dirt box. He didn't pay attention to the pointing dancers when the bass, in a bad moment, let out a birdlike squawk. Nor did he pay attention to the sight of Boner laughing—his head bent down, his rounded shoulders twitching behind the mixing board.

Mean One set his mind on higher things that night, thinking about the old jazz greats who passed through these rooms on their way to somewhere else—Stan Kenton, Glenn Miller, the Duke—and all those other cats like Pops who managed to swing in their own time inside these walls.

He thought about how their fingers struggled to find the notes, how they lugged equipment in and out of these rooms, shuffling their feet on the dusty floors, cold and alone before the dancers came. Like him, they had women waiting for them at home, and women waiting backstage.

And Mean One thought of the long drives at the end of each night, the salt from sweat like a thin film on their skin as they drove off, just a few dollars more than nothing in their pockets.

As he banged out song after song, he wondered about all the notes that had been played in the dance hall. How some were played beautifully and some badly. And he thought about how they were all still sounding there that night, ricocheting off the walls, ringing in a way that only certain ears could hear.

THE MANY SHORT TEETH
OF THE MANY LONG ZIPPERS

What thrilled her that night at the White Eagle Ballroom, what kept her trotting backstage, yelling to the band to play one more solo, was the very subtle crack overlooking the men's bathroom.

She had been innocently scanning the backstage wall when she discovered the slight opening just left of the vintage Andrews Sisters autograph that read "Get Happy" in a flowing insistent hand. She saw light shining through—and, voilà, there on the other side were many penises in a row, all making water.

Perhaps this is how Lewis and Clark felt when they came upon the Pacific Ocean. One day you're muddling through so much uncharted territory when you spy a break in the horizon and in the distance are the waters of an ocean so vast that people have only imagined it existed. At a moment like that the world opens up to you.

It's not like she was boy crazy, not like her friend Maria,

who claimed that when she saw large groups of men in public, she had the impulse to put out her hand and say, "I'll take that one, and that one, and that one," like she was choosing flavors at Donutland. It wasn't like that at all.

What thrilled her that night, what kept her coming back to the peephole to watch the steady stream of flies being undone, was the fact that she got to watch. Being watched, having your every jiggle and bounce noted and commented on, was an occupational hazard for the singer. But that night, she got to be the watcher. She got to gaze with interest.

First, she noticed how some men leaned forward, pressing their hand to the wall for support, peeing with exhaustion as if leaving behind a long list of grievances, while other men leaned back with drunken exultation, smiling and losing track of their streams, sending them wandering far off target. At last she understood one of life's great mysteries—why men's bathrooms smell so bad.

She noted with interest the subtle post-urination maneuver, the slight jiggle that men used to rid themselves of the last stubborn drop that never falls of its own accord. Of course the singer had known about penises, had seen them in all shapes, sizes, colors, and degrees of hardness and softness. It's not like she was naive.

But that night she realized in a new way that behind every man's zipper there lay a penis which was at times simply full of water and aching to be set free of its burden. This was a revelation.

And with this new knowledge, she watched as the men came and went. Onstage the band played the same tired guitar solos, and inside the bathroom, men sighed with regret as they finished up. Dipping their hips and hoisting themselves back into their pants, they zipped up the many short teeth of the many long zippers of the many pairs of pants walking around that night at the White Eagle Ballroom.

Smokes

They were surprised, she thought, to see her pull up in the old Nova they had given her when she went away to college. College hadn't lasted long, but the car still ran.

The Nova gasped to a halt in their driveway. Her mother and father crowded the foyer, peering out the open doorway. They stepped onto the stoop with their hands at their sides, as if they were afraid she might come in and try to sell them a vacuum cleaner.

They had not seen her for two years. No letters, no phone calls, not even at Christmas. Inside, the house looked just as it had when she left—the Magnavox in the far corner, the brown velvet couch along the long wall. On the backrest of the La-Z-Boy was the familiar oil spot from her father's hair tonic where he rested his head for afternoon naps.

She began to tell them about all the places she had visited in her two years of touring. The twenty-seven states, at last count. "One state for every year of my life," she joked in silence as they sat on the couch watching her, their hands resting in their laps.

She started to tell them about Shaky Jake, the harmonica player she had played with who left a growing wet spot on the right thigh of his jeans where he banged the water out of his harps every night, and she almost told them about Spike Malone, the guitarist who got his name from the leather spiked wristbands he wore on stage.

They didn't care to hear about the tourist sites she'd visited on her days off between gigs—the Washington Monument, the Grand Canyon. These places existed for them only as glossy pictures in books, as remote and abstract as she had become to them.

"We'll give you a long rope," her father said, when he finally did say something to her that last time she went home. "Long enough to hang yourself with."

After the supper dishes were cleared, they sat in the living room, her mother chattering away about her volunteer work, her father watching the TV with little interest, flipping through the channels. And the coldness of his profile, his eyes trained on the TV and his ear turned deafly to her, told her everything he would never say—that he did not approve of her roaming around the country in a van with a bunch of men.

She spent the rest of the weekend in her old bed trying to recreate the warm feeling of childhood, but her mother had cleared away her personal belongings and stored them in boxes in the basement for the time when she would have a real place of her own. Her old bedroom was now a guest room with crisp doilies on the dresser and designer dolls with large glass eyes staring at her from the shelves. Her old room was as clean and stripped of personal meaning as any of the hundreds of motel rooms she'd slept in over the past two years.

On Sunday, she packed her bags and loaded them in the car. She was behind the wheel, almost ready to pull out of the driveway, when her father leaned down as if to kiss her, but instead slipped a tightly folded fifty-dollar bill into her hand. She started to cry then, wanting to tell him everything—how she hadn't been paid her fair share, how they had taken off with the equipment, how one of them had been a married man—but only tears came out.

"Don't tell your mother," her father said, tapping her palm where the bill was nestled. Then he stood up straight and slapped the fender of the rusting car as if it were a palomino he was releasing into the wild.

Here at last is the short end of the long rope her father warned her she would eventually come to. The fifty-dollar bill has been gone for months, and the Nova no longer runs. At first the brakes, then the tires, then the transmission went. After that the ignition began to let out a little whine when she turned the key, so she pushed the car to a lot behind Freddie's house, where she sometimes crashes between gigs.

Freddie's place is a big falling-down house in what used to be a good neighborhood. No one knows how Freddie got the house and no one knows how he keeps it. Some things it's better not to ask. Inside are many rooms filled with old tattered couches and bare mattresses that he scavenges from curbsides. If your car makes it to Freddie's, there's always a place to crash.

It's a hot August day and Freddie has no air-conditioning. The only thing they can do is sit on the couch, sweat, and smoke. But now even the pack is empty.

"I'll fly," she offers, thinking sweat equity, thinking she has no money to buy.

"Nope," Freddie says. He's broke, too, or temporarily without means as he likes to put it, tugging at his T-shirt like it's a silk smoking jacket.

This is how they find themselves in her stalled-out Nova. By late afternoon, the sun has filled the car with a heat that feels like lava when they open the door. The vinyl seats sear her skin when she kneels on them to check the glove compartment for money.

They swing open all four doors to cool the car, and they take turns digging their thin fingers into the cushions between the cracks, saying *ouch, ouch,* looking for some small piece of silver she may have dropped during those salad days when the gas tank was full.

The sweat drips into Freddie's eyes. "Arrgh," he growls with disgust. He dips his hands deep in the cushions, fishing out guitar picks, bottle caps, clotted ballpoint pens, a few pennies. He places all this debris on the car seat, along with a growing wad of lint that looks suspiciously like mattress stuffing.

"Mouse nests?" she asks, shuddering to think of how close her Nova is to returning to the elements.

"Nah," he says, "car toe jam." He swats the back of his

ear for the fly that's buzzing by. "Scientifically proven to collect in abandoned Novas."

Eventually they give up and decide to bum four smokes
from the neighbor—two for her, two for Freddie. Then they
go inside and retrieve the last can of tender peas from the
deepest corner of Freddie's kitchen cupboard. It's old and
expired, like his grandmother who gave it to him as starter
foodstuff when he left home years ago. By now they've eaten
their way to the back of the pantry, through the pickles and
the candied yams.

"I guess it's Donner-party time," Freddie says, walking
close behind her, making a show of eyeing her neck.

She opens the peas, finds a pan, and turns on the
burner. When the coil begins to glow, he leans forward with
the cigarette and turns his face to the burner. He drags hard
and pulls the flame into the tip. Then he straightens his
back against the kitchen counter, blowing a thick trail of
smoke and watching her stir the peas.

Soon the neighborhood cat comes to the window meow-
ing. She's very pregnant, and they like having her around
because it makes them feel like someone is in a deeper
world of hurt than them.

The cat navigates the kitchen counter, tender-footed and
agile even in her advanced state. She lets out a tortured
meow from deep in her body and rubs her head against the
dishwasher, the toaster, the kitchen chairs marking everything with her scent.

"Oh, hell," Freddie says magnanimously, "give puss
some too."

They pour three steaming bowls of peas, and then go

into the living room to eat—the cat standing on the coffee table, her tail high in the air, her head bobbing as she ravenously takes in the tender green nuggets. After the cat is finished, she sits demurely on her hind quarters and licks her paws, her stomach billowing out as she lifts her back paw and stretches her jaw to clean all her deep and hidden places.

Freddie reclines on the couch and lights another cigarette. "Uh, uh, uh," he sings under his breath, blowing a smoke ring. "Sum, sum, summertime."

Tomorrow, she thinks, she will take out a piece of paper and write a letter to her father admitting, in thin pencil lines, that he was right. She imagines how the words will appear on the page, light and barely readable, written by a weak and defeated hand.

She'll lick the envelope and mail it with her last stamp. Then she will take up the short end of that long rope, and do one final trick with it—something that will stun and amaze them all.

She watches Freddie exhale the last drag of his cigarette. He picks up his guitar and sings a song about a pregnant veggie-eating cat with excellent hygiene, making up the words as he goes along. She laughs and sings with him each time he comes around to the chorus, *All we are saying, is give peas a chance.*

It's early in the evening and she still has two smokes left. She intends to suck them down clean to the filter.

Do Drop Inn

When they found Keith in a motel room in Jacksonville, someone said, they had to break the chain, throw a shoulder against the dark splinter of wood, force the metal rings to give up the mounted gold clasp. Someone else said the links were swinging free and the police walked into an already open door.

Doesn't matter except to know he wasn't alone in the end. Jacksonville's hot this time of year. Keith would've hated going in a mom-and-pop Do Drop Inn with a marquee flashing, *Eat, Sleep, Bowl*.

Those hands could play the three-over-four, the slide, the strut, the syncopation, like nobody could teach. He was always going to California, but first the dirty dance halls, then the pregnant wife, after that the fat paychecks on the cocktail circuit held him, always in debt, but on the way out and going to California shortly thereafter.

When I first met him, I had a habit of quitting smoking for twenty minutes, and he would vow to leave his wife. In that room where they found him, I imagine a woman slipping out from under and collecting her clothes. She slides the chain free and runs down the hallway, falling apart as she runs, falling apart as she runs away from Keith and the way he knew how to play.

SANTIAGO'S DEAD

It's more than rain
that falls on our parade tonight

TOM WAITS

The morning after Santiago, the woman wakes to the sound of the man singing in the shower, his unruly bass filtering through the rush of water. It's Puccini. She recognizes it from the needle-lifting drill he's been using to prepare for his music history comprehensive. One minute it's the acrobatic fingering of Mozart, then the unrelenting mathematical precision of Bach, after that Debussy's scattered noodlings, each one interrupted by the clumsy scratch of a needle. For weeks she has suffered through the needle-lifting drill—the scratchy records, the bellowing basses, the shrill sopranos.

Each night as she lies in bed reading, the ghosts of western music drift up the steps in fragments and gather in her ears. There they congregate—Grieg, Rachmaninoff, Chopin—

she can't not listen. At times she feels like jumping from the bed and screaming like a game show contestant, "I can name that tune in three notes!" She recalls reading how prisoners of war are sometimes tortured by their captors like this, with an incessant barrage of noise in the background. And so, she thinks, this is what they have come to.

A few nights earlier when he was in the basement practicing guitar, she got out of bed and slid down the hallway into the living room. Noiselessly feeling the contours of the wall with her hands, she listened for an interruption in the man's practice scales. For his comprehensives, the man is learning the Greek modes, the source of tonal music. Late at night, after he's lifted the needle for hours and practiced his chops on the trumpet, he retires to their windowless basement to practice the strange twisting scales of the Aeolian and Myxolydian modes on guitar.

That night the exotic sounds wound up the stairs as the woman quietly moved across the living room, careful to avoid the creaky spots in the wood floor. The room was dark except for a small glow from the night-light by the kitchen sink. In the semidarkness, she knelt before the man's record collection, her fingers scanning each album jacket as if she were searching for E5 on an old-fashioned jukebox.

Of all their friends, they were the only ones who still admitted to owning vinyl and even stored it, on full display, in their living room. Most of their friends saw this as proof that they belonged together—two doomed dinosaurs. The man refused to buy a CD player, declaring that, like beta tapes and eight-track players, CDs were a passing fad.

As the woman picked through the man's record collection, she listened for a break in his noise. She pictured him downstairs in his straight-backed chair, fingers running endlessly up and down the length of his guitar neck.

She found the record she wanted, Wagner's *Ring* operas. She removed it from the record sleeve and balanced the smooth black platter carefully in her right hand, as she soundlessly slipped one of her own albums, Devo's *Duty Now for the Future,* into the Wagner sleeve.

This felt so good that she searched further, replacing his copy of Tchaikovsky's *Pathétique* with her copy of Pink Floyd's *Ummagumma.* Then she exchanged Mozart's *Requiem* with U2's *Rattle and Hum.* She had spent the next thirty minutes, her eyes getting more and more accustomed to the dim light, mixing and matching until she ran out of appropriate combinations. This done, she had climbed the stairs happily, ready for a good night of sleep, barely noticing the haunting sounds winding up the staircase behind her.

But lying in bed this morning listening to the man's rousing opera, she realizes that the switch had been made days ago and still she has heard nothing from him—no response, not even angry silence. Instead, this morning he is loitering noisily under the rush of water, bent on singing the entire score of *Madame Butterfly.*

Here comes the tragic recurring motif, the complaining whine of the soprano circling back like a carrion bird, reminding the listener that trouble lurks somewhere in the composition, always threatening to return. The sounds come through the warble of water, the man reaching for the high note. Something catches in his throat. He gropes and fails, then drops an octave to finish the vocal line in defeat.

"Amateur." The woman kicks her covers off.

She has a secret hatred of casual singers—the lady standing behind her at the checkout humming along with the Muzak, her boss who whistles Christmas carols all year long except at Christmastime. She hates them all and wishes they would keep their badly sung notes to themselves, these hummers, these through-the-teeth whistlers, these under-the-breath singers.

The man is in the bathroom singing and shaving now. She can hear the vowels rise and fall, tighten and loosen according to the position of the razor on his neck.

"Are you finished yet?" she yells, pulling the sheets off the bed.

The buzz of the razor continues. The man appears not to have heard. This makes her more angry. She feels a small hot redness rise through her body. It's hardly fair. Each morning she's the one who has to go to work, but he's the one who spends hours in the bathroom.

The woman lifts the corner of the waterbed mattress and tucks a clean sheet underneath. A musty odor rises—the smell of plastic like a new doll, and under that, a faint trace of something moldy. For months she's been trying to find the origin of the smell. Already she has torn down the bed from where it stood for seven years.

Under the pedestal she expected to find a small, half-rotten mouse, but when she unhinged the boards and ran her fingers through the nap, she found nothing, just the yellow carpet, bright and unmatted, looking considerably better than where the carpet had been walked on for years. The woman had bleached the bedding and wiped down the mattress, but when the bed was reassembled, the smell had returned.

In the bathroom, the buzz of the razor subsides and the man continues to hum lightly. She listens for the click of the bathroom door and the sound of the man's feet padding down the steps. At last. She looks at the clock—fifteen minutes to get ready for work.

In the bathroom, she brushes her teeth and pulls off her pajamas, turning the nozzle to start the shower. Checking the temperature of the water with her fingertips, she gingerly steps into the shower. How she hates getting wet. She secretly believes she was a cat in another life. The water swirls heavily down her face and back, reminding her of the whirlpool that pulls at her in sleep.

Often in the middle of the night, she is caught like this in the center of a large, shallow lake, and no matter how hard she swims she cannot find shore. She spins madly and flails her arms and legs, but she gets nowhere. When awake, she is terrified of water and cautious around it. She would never willingly go into it. But in the dream, she swims beautifully at first, her long strokes reaching ahead of her body. Soon enough, pain ripples through every muscle. The greedy weeds love her feet. They pull her down, her long hair spiraling after her, her lungs growing heavy and full.

And this is what usually wakes her, as it had last night—the feeling of something tight around her throat. When she opened her eyes the man was sitting next to the bed.

"What?" she had said, thinking he said something. The word sputtered from her lungs.

"Honey," he said quietly, as if he had some very bad

news. His long dark hair hung over his eyes. The outline of his body in the darkness scared her.

"What?" she repeated. It was the only word she could manage. It seemed to blare from her. In the dim bedroom she saw only his silhouette and a thin haze surrounding his body.

"Santiago's dead," the man said, taking her limp hand and putting it to his lips.

Santiago was the last in a long line of Siamese fighting fish the couple had owned. This species of fish had a warrior nature and could not occupy a tank with its own kind. When the man and the woman first started living together, they embraced this as a romantic notion—being hopelessly drawn to, but repelled by, one of your own species.

"I played guitar for him for an hour," the man said, "but he just stopped swimming." He sat on the bed, his hands lying useless in his lap. "He just went to the surface and stopped swimming."

"I know," the woman said, fully awake now. "I know." She patted his back.

Santiago was not the first fish to die in their tanks. The first one had been named Blue, but the woman had killed him—not on purpose, of course—an accident, something to do with the acid-alkaline balance in the water. Santiago had come much later, after Blue, after they had set up the second tank and started keeping the fish in pairs with names such as Zelda and F. Scott, who succeeded Zelda, then came Ahab who outlasted F. Scott, then Ishmael and Noah, then much, much later, there was Papa who went though Hadley and Pauline and countless others until Santiago came along. No one had outlasted Santiago.

"Jesus," the woman whispered, lifting herself up in the bed. Through the window she could see the globe of the streetlight and the thin rings of light surrounding it. "What time is it?"

"Three o'clock," the man said, bending over and resting his head on her chest, his long black hair streaming across her blanket. "I didn't mean to wake you, but I knew you would want to know about it right away."

It's true, the woman thinks the next morning as she shampoos her hair, the lather rising and spilling onto her forehead and into her eyes—she did want to know. Santiago was their champion, the one who had lasted the longest. But she also knows it is only an excuse, like all the other excuses the man has used over the years to wake her.

At first there were the small knocking noises in the middle of the night that he didn't understand and was worried about. And then there were the times when the water heater ran out of hot water and he had to wake her to find out the landlord's phone number.

Sometimes there were late-night TV specials about the mating rituals of animals, which always made him lonely for her. And the missing tools that he desperately needed, and he was sorry to wake her but she was always putting things away in places where he couldn't find them.

Often she woke to the sound of the vacuum passing like a phantom over the living room carpet, which, in the darkest hour of the night, had become inexcusably dirty. And more recently, she has woken to the pungent hiss of bug spray assaulting her nostrils, two floors up. If she rises from bed and slips into the basement quietly, she will catch him furiously exterminating the hordes of roaches, water bugs, and silverfish that seem to make their appearance only after midnight.

Then there are the fish. Every two of three months there are the dying-in-the-middle-of-the-night fish. The man has a need for all these excuses because in all the years they have lived together the man has not slept—that is to say, the man has never come upstairs to bed and slept—and there are still those nights that are too long and too dark, even for him.

The woman gets out of the shower and dresses quickly for work. She is already late. No time for breakfast. She finds the man downstairs, sitting in the lotus position drying his hair. Posted on either side of him like sentinels are two box fans blowing on their highest setting.

Today is not a hot day, but every day the man insists on running the fans. He is uncomfortable in the humidity and has never forgiven the woman for luring him into this humid climate. Every morning when she leaves for work he reminds her of this by quoting the relative humidity and the current barometric pressure off the Weather Channel, stating it matter-of-factly like it's all her doing.

This morning she finds him scanning a textbook on the late Romantic period while he runs the blow-dryer up and down the length of his long hair. *Gilligan's Island* is blaring loudly above the sound of the fans.

"Bad night?" she sits down on the couch.

"What?" he says, his voice wavering as if from inside a wind cave.

The woman eyes the textbook nervously. The man uses a complex highlighting system for studying. In it, proper nouns and important dates are marked in yellow; significant events are marked in pink; theories, laws, and rules are marked in green; and the rest of the text is glossed over in blue, because blue is his favorite color.

"I have a doctor's appointment today," the woman announces, hoping to draw his attention away from the book and all of its markings. It makes her nervous—him poking in his books. A few weeks earlier, when she was sick and stayed home from work, she had taken down his books and traced over the highlighting system, making new colors—mauves, oranges, purples—and then placed the books back on the shelves just to see if he'd notice. So far he hadn't said anything, and she doesn't have time for a confrontation this morning.

"Could you turn that down, please," the woman says, motioning to the TV. She gets up and turns the fans down to a mild hum.

"Bad night?" she asks again, hoping he'll hear this time. She notices his eyes are tired and redder than usual. On the end table beside the couch are the two fish tanks, empty now, the water cloudy with parasites that are still flourishing in the water. Parasites, the woman thinks, that have not yet been informed the host is dead.

"I can't do this anymore," the man says finally, turning over his textbook.

"Do what?" The woman asks, anxiously.

"That." The man points to the countertop where Santiago waits in a little bundle. "I can't stand losing them."

"Let's give it a few days," she says. "Time to clear the tanks, time for the parasites to kill each other off." The woman bends over and pecks the man on the top of his head. "Let's take a few days to think about it."

"He's over there," the man says softly, motioning once again toward the kitchen counter. Since he's the one who fishes the bodies out of the water in the middle of the night, he's the one who must prepare them for burial, wrapping them in paper towels. He can't bear the thought of flushing them down the toilet like ordinary goldfish. He makes the woman take the corpses to work and bury them in an open field outside her office building.

"I've got to go," she says, getting up and going to the counter. She balances the featherweight of Santiago on her palm.

"Twenty-one-point-nine today," the man says, quoting the barometer as the woman opens the door to the humid spring morning.

On her way to the car, she stops at the dumpster and slips Santiago under some discarded boxes of soiled diapers and empty baby food jars. With her long arms, she reaches in deep, so that the man will have no chance of finding him.

He came to live with her after their affair, after his wife found the letters they continued to write after their affair. He appeared one day with a U-haul and one hundred dollars, ringing the doorbell and standing on her front steps stunned and bewildered.

He came filled with stories of how happy he had been with his wife, not knowing it, of course, until it was too late.

He rattled on about his wife so much that she became a presence in their lives, a guiltless, long-suffering angel. She was everywhere—in the special recipes they cooked, which he had called her on the phone to get when he began to miss the taste of her cooking. She was present in the thick layer of dust that landed on the knickknacks he had pulled dust-free from the boxes she had so perfectly packed for him. The man loved to tell stories of the happy years he had spent in their first apartment, which his ex-wife had decorated entirely in blue because blue was his favorite color.

That's how the woman came to find the blue fish for their new apartment. At the mall one day, scanning the windows for something blue to buy to comfort him, she saw the Siamese fighting fish floating in a tank in the store window, their blue fins streaming off their bodies like Chinese silk.

"They're beautiful," the woman said, going inside to observe them more closely. She took her time, selecting the best pair, then asking the attendant to put them in a bag for her and to recommend a tank that would work for the two of them.

"No can do," the attendant said. He was enjoying his gum considerably.

"No can do?" she asked. She hadn't realized people still used phrases like that.

"Nope. You gotta have separate tanks for these babies. Otherwise they'll pulverize each other." When he said the word *pulverize* a little bit of spit shot out of his mouth and landed on the counter.

"All's I know," he said, leaning forward confidentially, "is they bet on them in Japan or Thailand somewhere. You know, like in cock fights."

"So when you put them in a tank together?" the woman asked.

"They pulverize each other." He smiled. "See this." He reached under the counter and produced a large hand mirror.

"It doesn't even have to be another fish," the attendant explained. "Just his own reflection will get him going." He went to the fish tank and pressed the mirror up against its flat surface. Immediately when the blue fish spotted himself in the mirror, his fins spread wide like an oriental fan. His gills rose in a tight blossom around his neck. He hung there very still in the water, guarding the perimeter for any sign of a possible attack.

"That's why they call 'em Siamese fighting fish," the attendant said. "Poor suckers don't even know their own reflections."

They watched as the fish held and improved his stance. He inhaled, pumping himself up, a preening lone warrior suspended in water. He reminded the woman of those weight lifters in bodybuilding competitions who struggle in the final round to outposture the rest of the field, maneuvering their way to the front row with their muscles rippling.

"How long could this go on?" the woman asked.

"Oh, all day, all night." The attendant shrugged. "Just as long as they see that reflection." He removed the mirror and the fish relaxed immediately and fantailed his way to the corner of the tank.

"So you want one or not," the attendant said, tired of her questions, wanting to close the sale. "I could fix you up with a mixture."

"No," the woman said quickly. "No mixture. Just one blue fish and a large tank to go with him."

On the drive home that day so many months ago, the woman had been excited. She could not wait to get home and set up the tank, to put in the little white rocks for the bottom and hook up the bubbling replica of the Shaolin temple. When that was done, she would drop the fish in and call the man upstairs to show him the first blue thing she had found.

The day after Santiago, the woman perches on an examination table waiting for the doctor to arrive who will give her a name for the illness that's been traveling around inside her. Already she's missed several days of work, and lately she walks around feeling tired and generally not well.

As the woman waits, she admires the cleanliness of the walls and listens to the hum of the fluorescent light overhead. Her clothes hang limply on a peg on the wall. The stainless steel instruments lined up in a neat row wait quietly on the movable table beside her.

The pain has a traveling quality. Some days it's an ache in the left breast, some days a tight pinch in her right side. An elusive pain, it always migrates to a part of the body that is not handled by the specialist she is seeing that day.

As she waits, the woman fantasizes about the name of her disease. It will be a long word, no doubt, difficult to spell, nearly impossible to pronounce. It will ring fatally from the doctor's lips, perhaps taking two or even three doctors all working together to fully articulate it.

"Aneurysm," the woman rolls the word around her

tongue, the vowels gliding and shifting like too many mar-
bles in her mouth. "An-e-ur-y-sm," the woman sounds it
out, all those vowels set to unravel wildly on contact.

"Cancer," the woman continues, trying out the few
words for diseases she knows. Of course there are millions
of names for diseases she does not know.

"Cancer," she cracks the *k* sound like a hard nut with
her jaw.

She often has a dream that she's in an operating room
surrounded by doctors with masks. In the dream she watches
them work from above even though she's fully anesthetized.
They look like coal miners with their face masks and overhead lights. They work through the night, yelling for scalpels
and clamps, finally opening her up. "Full of cancer." They
shake their heads and click their tongues with regret.

"What a shame," they say, "nothing more to be done for
her." They close her up and send her home.

"Melanoma." Here's another word the woman fears, although it sounds harmless enough, more like a passing bad
mood than a lethal dose of skin cancer. "Polyps," she pops
the *p*, imagining polyps growing like wild mushrooms in
her large intestine.

She stays there as instructed, like a good patient, poised
between the stirrups on the padded bed. The paper gown
they have given her has no backside, and when she shifts
her weight she rips the disposable paper on the bed beneath her.

No worry, the woman thinks. The paper comes off a roll
at the head of the bed. When she's gone, the nurse will come
in and tear off the ruined length and prepare the room for

the next person. It will be as though she's never been there.

"Well, you're not dying." The doctor knocks and enters. Over the last several months he has voiced his concerns to this woman, so obviously healthy, who insists they run test after test on her. This year alone she's had blood tests, urine tests, a liver analysis, X rays, and a series of breast exams in which a mysterious lump she claimed to own proved to be nonexistent. The doctor has probed her orifices, poked her gall bladder, listened to her lungs, checked her blood pressure, taken her temperature, and in all that time has found nothing substantially wrong with her.

"Well, we did find something unusual today," the doctor says.

"What?" the woman asks, relieved.

"It appears you are pregnant," the doctor announces, surprising even himself.

"Jesus," the woman says, staring at her purple toenails. "How could that be?" These days, moments of intimacy were rare, and when they did occur, they were rushed and frantic, more like wrestling matches than lovemaking. She presses her forehead, struggling to recall their last encounter.

"Well, it only takes once," the doctor reminds her, "and only one little swimmer out of millions."

"Yeah, but what are the odds of that?" she asks. "I mean, the last time that happened didn't a star rise in the east."

"Not exactly," the doctor says, grinning as he bends to finish the report. "Come back next week and we'll do a full workup." Opening the door, he drops her chart in the holder outside the door.

✦

Some days, if she has time, on the way home from work, she likes to take the old road that follows the river, gently winding around the north side of town. Today the trees are beautiful. They are still bare from the long winter, but the breeze is warm and she drives with her windows open.

Most days she likes to look at the quaint little houses with their miniature lawn ornaments—reindeer, toads, homemade windmills—and wonder what life must be like inside those houses. Sometimes she imagines what it would be like to have a garden and a clothesline and a real pet, something bigger than a fish.

If she lived in a house like those on River Road she would lock the doors at night, shut off the lights, and go to sleep in the total quiet—no stereo, no guitar, no TV playing late into the night—and always there would be someone next to her in the bed. Perhaps they would sit and read together, talking a bit before they took off their reading glasses and fell asleep. The last sound would be the click of the bedside lamp.

She thinks again about being pregnant—it must have been some prodigious sperm that made the terrific climb up all those carpeted stairs from the basement to the upstairs bedroom. This is the only way it could have happened, she reasons, since she spends her time upstairs reading, and he spends his nights in the basement working on his beloved manuscript.

Nothing has ever taken him away from his work. "In this book I hope to explain everything that's happened to the guitar in the last one hundred years," he had said when he moved in with her. She'd sat on the living room floor that night in awe of him, just taking in the shape of his face, watching the way the light glanced off his features. It was an ambitious goal, she knew, but she had encouraged him. She couldn't believe he had actually come to be with her.

In the seven years they'd been together he'd written chapters on everyone from Segovia and Chuck Berry to Jimmy Page and Villa-Lobos, including Julian Bream and Yngwie Malmsteen. A monumental task, she knew, and all of it done in the deepest part of the night.

Each night as she went to bed alone, downstairs he hunched over the stereo playing a record at sixteen revolutions, the slowest speed, so he could transcribe famous guitar solos for his book. Returning the needle to the record again and again, he agonized over each nuance as the notes moaned off the record an octave lower than normal, sounding demonic and tortured to the woman trying to sleep in the bedroom upstairs.

But had it always been this way? How had they gotten here—retired to separate floors? She thinks back to the beginning. The day after she accidentally killed their first fish, Blue, she had returned to the pet store to pick out another blue fish. She'd also picked out a red one that day, and a second tank so that the blue fish wouldn't be so lonely.

"See what it says about the red ones," the woman asked the man that night as she finished the dishes. He had been scouring the fish manuals all evening for clues as to what had brought about Blue's demise.

"Let's see, color," he said, flipping through the index. "It says they breed them in Thailand for the color. It takes many years—thousands of generations of very blue females and very blue males."

"And the red ones?" the woman asked.

"Same goes for them," the man said absentmindedly.

"That's a lot of lives of a lot of fish," the woman said, trying to imagine a thousand generations.

"It would go fast if they belonged to you," the man said, looking up at the woman. "Murderer," he hissed.

"I didn't kill him on purpose." The woman slammed down a dish and turned quickly. "I swear." She wiped her hands on the dish towel. "Tell me again how it is they mate," she said, coming into the living room and sitting down beside him. She wanted to hear the dangerous part close up.

"Well." The man set his book down. This part he knew by heart. "They drop the female into the tank and hope that he doesn't kill her."

"Really," the woman said, giggling already.

"Of course," the man said, fingering her buttons. "The females are very plain and not much of a threat." He looked up. "Just like in all the other species."

The woman slugged him in the arm. "Just like in some of the other species."

"Yeah, yeah," the man said. "And then before she knows what hit her," the man sat up and grabbed the woman's legs, pushing them tight to her chest, "he pounces on her."

"Oh, I love that part." The woman laughed. "And then what happens?"

"Well," he said, breathless from the effort of holding her down. "Then he's gotta kill her." He moved closer and nuzzled her neck.

"And the little ones? What becomes of them?"

"If he's hungry," he said, very close to her ear, "he eats them."

"Oh, you." She struggled to get out of his arms. That's the part she couldn't understand. With the males killing each other, and the females and the offspring getting maimed and eaten, how did they perpetuate their species? Later, when she read the fish manual herself, she found that the key was in the water. In their natural habitat the water was murky—the females got away, the children grew up. The deadly males swam right by each other in the dim water, often unaware of each other's presence.

The evening after Santiago, the woman parks the car and enters the apartment quietly. She hopes the man will be downstairs working. Normally, she can count on not seeing him at all, but today she's been to the mall and has several packages. The man worries constantly about money. Even though she makes it, he doesn't like her to spend it. He has excellent shopping hearing. She swears he can hear her coming two blocks away when she has bags crinkling in the car. She's halfway up the steps when he appears behind her.

"What'd you buy?" he asks.

"Oh, nothing," she says, hurrying up the steps.

"Well, you got something."

"Just some stuff on sale," she says, relieved when he doesn't follow her.

"We've got to talk," the man yells from the foot of the stairs.

"About what?" The woman stops at the landing and looks back.

"Never mind, now," the man says, motioning downstairs

to where his work waits for him. "Maybe later."

"Yeah, maybe," she says, turning the corner into the bedroom.

She unpacks the bags, pulling out the oversized blouses. She'll soon be needing these. She gets out a high stool and reaches into the top shelf of her closet, bringing down a suitcase. She folds and places the maternity blouses inside the suitcase and returns the bag to its high shelf.

Then she digs through the shopping bags for the novel she bought at the mall. It's a book she's been meaning to read for a long time. "The greatest fish story ever," the man said when he named Santiago after the main character, "told by a great fisherman."

Throughout the evening, as the woman reads, she hears the ghostly wail of voices from the man's stereo downstairs. Later in the evening he moves upstairs to the living room, turning the TV up to a blare and grinding out scale after scale on his guitar. All night the twisted remnants of the Lydian and Ionian modes drift up the steps. She continues to read the fish novel late into the night. It is a short book, cleanly written. But, the woman thinks, it's not a fish story at all.

If the author of this book were still alive, he would argue that she's much like the ladies of his time who attended bullfights—always worried about the bulls and the horses, never properly concerned about the toreadors. And it's true. The woman finds herself irresistibly drawn to the marlin and not to the old man. The fish is at home in the water, she reasons. At best the old fisherman is a poorly behaved visitor.

The woman reads the fish story, wanting the whole time

for the fish to stop swimming relentlessly out to sea and to recognize the hook in its mouth. She knew what the fish did not understand—that if he were to retrace the line, it would lead back to the hands of the man who insisted on calling him "brother" while killing him.

When the old man says, "Don't go deep, fish," the woman whispers, "Go deep, fool, go deep." And when the old man says, "Come up now, friend, fill your lungs with air," the woman begs the fish not to believe that word *friend* coming from the fisherman's lips. But the fish doesn't listen. He and the old man are bound together in the pattern of a story not of her making. And all that is left for her, the reader, is to watch the design play out.

"Every story, if told to its natural conclusion, ends tragically," the author of the fish book once wrote. "And he is no true storyteller who tells you differently."

After the woman finishes the story, straight through to its devastating end, she cannot sleep. She notices that downstairs the TV is blasting, but the man has fallen silent. The woman gets out of bed and goes downstairs. There she finds him stretched out on the floor, the guitar lying next to him. She turns the TV off and gets a thin blanket from the closet to cover him. He blinks and swallows in his sleep, breathing deeply into the dark night.

He's not dreaming of her, she knows. She imagines he dreams of the ample curve of his guitar, of running his fingers as swiftly as possible over the smoothness of its neck, playing in the Phrygian, playing in the Dorian mode.

She tiptoes down the stairs to his basement workroom. There she finds his dissertation spread out on his desk, the

neat stacks in rows chronicling the modern history of the
guitar. Under the black-and-white text of this history lies
another story. If spoken, its words would be uttered through
clenched teeth and would ring in a gravelly voice of their
lost seven years. But this is the story no one ever tells.

At first she contents herself with moving the chapters
around a bit, mixing them up, putting them in a random
and unexpected order. This simple act feels good. Next she
searches for the chapter on Black Sabbath and places it in
the chronological history before Segovia. Then she removes
Eric Clapton and replaces him with the notorious flamenco
player, Pepe Romero, as the original guitarist for Cream.

Now that was fun, she thinks. She looks further. Finding
the pages about Buddy Holly, she throws them into the trash.
She's always believed he was overrated anyway. It's amazing
how a tragic and untimely end will boost an artist's career.
She climbs up the two flight of stairs to her floor. In the bathroom, she breathes deeply into the quiet as she brushes her
teeth and washes her face. She likes the feel of the warm
washcloth scrubbing her skin, cleaning all of her pores.

In the bedroom she finds the fish book tangled between
the sheets. Riffling through the pages, she whispers to the
ghost of the fabulously famous author, "You're dead old man.
You don't write the ending anymore." She flips through the
book, searching for those few happy lines where Santiago,
however briefly, had a moment of triumph—after he catches
the marlin, before the sharks come to pick the carcass clean.

She rips these pages out of the book and reinserts them
somewhere near the beginning. Much better, she thinks. Now
the old man floats home easily with the fish lashed securely

to his skiff. Like two brave twins, the fish and the old man make the long journey, the wind in their sails, the sea keeping the boat buoyant beneath them.

Soon Santiago will wake and find it was all a dream. He has simply overslept and dreamt of catching the world-class marlin. Only in his dreams was he pulled into the blinding vastness of the ocean. At dawn the young village boy will come and wake him as usual, offering a bit of rice and the morning paper. The old man will rise unheroically as all men do, and sit for a time in his underwear, reading the paper and talking with the boy about American baseball and the great DiMaggio.

Even his old wife will still be alive, sleeping quietly beside him in the bed. When she rises to put water on for coffee, the old man will shake his head and tell the boy his strange dream. Perhaps then, in that quiet moment before the day truly begins, he will have the courage to confide his one great fear to the boy—that he will never again be a great fisherman.

"There, there, old man," the woman says quietly, standing on a chair and tucking the book onto the high shelf of her closet beside her suitcase. Inside her suitcase, something empty and full of possibility waits for her to bring it to new shape. The silence of the night reaches her. It is now very late.

The woman turns off the reading light and goes to the window. Everyone in the city is asleep. Breathing the cool spring air, she watches the streetlights glow and hiss. Strange, she thinks, how quiet it grows in the middle of the night.

RIDING SHOTGUN THROUGH IOWA WITH QUEST

This musician's life. Play until one o'clock, pack up, get paid. Send the dancers home drunk, sweaty, clinging to each other. On the long way home, I ride shotgun with Quest helping keep watch over the night.

Our talk turns to women and death, what Quest calls *all things inevitable*. He is not so afraid of the final embrace as the moment before, the arms stretched out to us, the looking into the eyes of it. In the dead of this night, we agree to trust it—the good faith of this road running beneath us.

I tell him how this place is like my home, where every night vapor lights burn in yards, and every morning farmers rise at dawn to milk the cows. Not for me, that life. In a family of settlers I was the emigrant, fixing my eye on the horizon, setting myself to reel madly across the continent.

Flying through Iowa, past cornfields and silos, the two-storied houses our dancers have gone to sleep in, I doze, wake, doze, to find Quest, hands on the wheel, trying to out-distance the road.

Five o'clock, passing a farmyard, I see my father step out to do the morning chores. His shadow, bending to pet the dog, becomes my brother.

This is the time of accidents—the ones we'll never see. We pass through twilight knowing that soon the sun will show its awful face, that soon even our headlights will be worthless.

Through the
Beaded Curtain

In the third grade I did very well in the screaming auditions for *Hansel and Gretel*. I got to be the witch. Oh sure, there were other girls who could yell louder and for longer periods of time, but the Sisters picked me because of the let's-put-the-mean-witch-in-the-oven scene.

I got the part because I was small enough to fit into the oven, but I had a scream that was big and mean and gritty and said, "I'm not just a kid in a black wig in here wrinkling crackly paper to make it sound like fire." It said, "I'm a goddamn for-real witch and I'm getting my fuckin' ass burned off in here." That's what I think it sounded like, looking back at it now.

First I had to compete against my best friend, Shelly Hildebrandt. She was a tall girl with a voice like a foghorn. She was a monster. On the playground you could see and hear her above everyone else. I knew that no matter how good she was, she was never going to fit into the oven, but the nuns went ahead and let her holler her head off anyway.

Next came Candy Schneider. She was small enough, but when she got up to the stage she just hunched over and whimpered in a little puny voice. "She's pathetic," Shelly nudged me with her big arm. I agreed. I had never seen a witch, but at least I knew what they sounded like. I knew they sounded mean like snake venom or something, and the nuns must have known that too because they sent Candy back to class.

We sat there for a while just sitting on our hands and kicking our feet, until the nuns called Bobby Fetzer's name. She walked up to the stage with her chest thrown way out in front of her. She stood there tugging at her dress and yelping every so often as if she were getting stung by a bee. We had to laugh then because it made us feel funny—all that howling—and every time she yelped, we jumped in our seats.

The elimination rounds went on like this forever, my throat getting more and more raw every time I was called up. Finally my voice started to sound thick and growly like some animal that was maybe wounded out there in the trees. I think that's when it started to make the nuns nervous. I noticed they leaned together and whispered into their hands every time I screamed.

I should have known then that I had a destiny, a *vocation*, as Father Kroeller used to call it every time he spoke to us about how we were all going to grow up to be priests and nuns. I should have known then that I had a vocation to be a rock-and-roll singer.

✦

My mother made me a witch costume for the part. It had a long flowing black skirt and a black blouse with puffy sleeves. We raided the Christmas decorations and spray painted some angel hair black. After it dried I pasted it to the hairnet and arranged the hair so that it fell in long strands down my shoulders. To complete the costume my dad got a broom from the hardware store, which the nuns told me I had to lose before I went into the oven. Otherwise, Hansel wouldn't be able to get the door closed.

I still have the photograph my mother took of me that night before we left for the performance. In the picture I'm standing in front of my house trying to look wicked. I'm straddling the broom like a Harley.

I have another picture, taken in the same spot one year later, after my mother turned the witch costume into a nun's habit for the school Halloween party. She only needed to replace the black wig with a long black handkerchief. I liked that much better because it flowed straight down my back and didn't smell or itch. Everything else stayed the same, except for the broom, which I had lost by then anyway.

That year, the year my witch's costume was converted into a nun's habit, I sang in public for the first time. There was a song called "Dominique" that was popular on the radio. This song had about thirty verses all recounting the wondrous feats of this character Dominique, who was a nomadic do-gooder. The chorus went something like this: *Domanique-anique-anique, over the land he plods along, and sings his little song. Never asking for reward, he just talks about the Lord. He just talks about the Lord.*

The radio version had been sung by a real nun, so the

Sisters, after seeing my nun's costume at Halloween, decided that I was to perform it for the Christmas concert. I had a hard time memorizing all those verses, but I felt confident because I knew that if I messed up I always had that rousing chorus to fall back on.

After the Christmas concert the Sisters carted me off to the Senior Citizens' Home, where I played to a real tough crowd, what with the infirmity and all. The next day I had to get dressed up again and sing "Dominique" to each individual class. By this time I was getting pretty sick of this song, and all those thirty verses, and especially I was getting sick of the way the sisters had instructed me to sing it: with my hands folded neatly in prayer and a devout look on my face.

By the time I got to the eighth graders, I was just about wishing that old Dominique had never lived, or if he had to live, that he would have stayed home a bit more. Thinking about it now, I know what the Sisters were doing. They were using me for recruiting purposes, you know—the world's youngest nun, and you could be one, too.

I've always been a singer. My whole family sang and, especially when I was young, I thought singing was something that everyone did, like eating and sleeping. When we drove to Bismarck, four times a year at the change of season, we always sang. But we didn't sing "Blue Suede Shoes" or "Good Golly, Miss Molly." We sang, *Whoops there goes another rubber tree plant, kerplunk,* and *Michael rowed the boat ashore, hallelujah.*

We also sang every Sunday night of the summer when my father herded us into the Chevy to look at the crops. We sang as we passed the waving rows of wheat; we sang to the orange sun dropping off into the horizon; but mostly, we sang for the ice cream we knew we were going to get at the Dairy Maid after we ran out of crops to look at.

In those days, rock and roll didn't impress me much, not even when my older sister took me to see *A Hard Day's Night*. I still remember the lime-green sleeveless shift she wore to the theater that night and the velveteen bow she had pinned into her beehive hairdo.

She sniffed and cried throughout the entire movie, digging for her hanky every five minutes or so. I wanted to ask her why she was crying. I wanted to ask her who the Beatles were, why they kept running from place to place and why people were always ripping their clothes off. They looked like nice enough boys, like they hadn't done anything wrong, and they were good singers too. I especially liked it when they did that high *oooh* stuff.

I had a recurring nightmare when I was a kid, about a little girl who had no home and slept on grates in the street. In the dream, the little girl wakes up and realizes she's me; then I wake up and realize that I am her. The Beatles reminded me of that dream—all that running around and no mom or dad in sight.

I have a theory about music, which I usually never take credit for because I think I may have read it somewhere and forgotten the source. I usually begin talking about this theory by saying, "I read somewhere about a study that was done," but I'm going to go on record now and say that I believe this is my own theory.

My theory, anyway, is that people become more suscep-
tible to music at certain times in their lives, such as the
times when they are courting and mating. Ask anyone what
song was playing on the radio the night they were driving
around and they got their first kiss or their first feel, and
they could probably tell you. It has a lot more to do with hormones than with music, but still the music gets remembered along with everything else.

For me, the important part of this theory is that the
music, whatever is popular or being played at the time, is
probably the music that people will keep with them for the
rest of their lives.

The empirical evidence I have to support this theory is
the fact that my parents have gone uptown every Saturday
night for the last forty years to dance the polka, which is perhaps the most unromantic dance known to man. Still, they
cling to this ritual. Their explanation: the polka is the dance
they did when they first started dating, and they've always
been able to do it well together. When they dance the polka,
they say, they glide on air.

I was ten when I started hearing rock and roll and distin-
guishing it from something other than the door slamming
or the toilet flushing. That summer, my parents hired a con-
struction crew to build a garage on our land. I remember
taking lemonade and cookies out to the tanned crew too
many times each afternoon, and I remember the way they
laughed and poked each other every time I showed up with
another tray of sweets.

I sat in the sun and watched the sweat trickle down their

shoulders. I watched them lift the frosty glasses with their large hands, and in the background the radio was playing songs of forbidden love: *I saw her again last night, but you know that I shouldn't.*

It started then, I believe, and even now every significant and insignificant event that remains crammed in my too-full-with-the-garbage-of-the-past mind is coupled with a memory of the music that was being played at the time.

Like the summer my brother played guitar for the Mystic Eyes and they practiced every night in our Quonset. They did all those songs that had double words for titles like "Louie, Louie" and "Mony, Mony." They did "Little Red Riding Hood" by Sam the Sham and the Pharaohs, and when the part came where everyone howls, I would lean out my window and *aaooh* right along with them.

I sat in my bedroom with the window wide open and listened to their lanky lead singer wail away for Gloria, an unknown girl he was never going to meet. Chanting over and over they sang *G-L-O-R-I-A*, the letters rising up and losing their order in the cool night air.

When I got a little older, old enough to ride around with men in cars, I remember a particular convertible in which my hair stood up straight from the rush of wind. Listening to Alice Cooper, we drove down the road singing, *Eighteen and I can do what I want, eighteen I just don't know what I want.* Or speeding home from a drive-in showing of *Easy Rider* in a pumpkin-orange Mustang one night, I remember everyone, including the people in the backseat, taking turns steering. Everyone singing at the top of their lungs, *Born to Be wild.*

✦

It went on like this for years, rock and roll ornamenting my life, a fixture no more or less significant than the turquoise wallpaper my mother had plastered on our walls. It was on a Sunday afternoon that I walked through the beaded curtain and the seduction occurred.

I remember the day but not the date. It was spring or fall, one of the transitional seasons. There was a party at Steve Benz's house. He was quite a few years older than me and he had been to Vietnam. Steve had always been wild, everyone knew that. Maybe that's how he survived the war. But after he came back he was different. He had a look of sheer mania. I had known he was a little crazy ever since one night when I was driving around with him and he sped up to hit a black cat that was scrambling across the street.

When I screamed, he slammed on the brakes and looked at me as if I had interrupted a sacrament. The look on his face was one hundred percent pure wild-eyed lunatic.

It was Steve who had gotten me stoned for the first time a few years earlier. I had smoked a few times, but all I felt was time slowing down and I hadn't liked that. When you grow up in a small town, the last thing you want to do is make time go more slowly.

One night Steve invited a carload of girls that I was driving around with to come out to the country and smoke something he had brought back from California. We drove out to a road about a half-mile from my parents' farm. Another car was already waiting for us. It was cold outside, so everybody packed into Steve's car.

We had nine, maybe ten people in this big green beast he was driving at the time. I think it was an Oldsmobile. I was sitting in the backseat on the laps of two guys a little older than me. My three girlfriends had piled in the front seat along with Steve.

The pipe went around. The car got smoky. It was hot in the car and humid. When I took a breath it spooked me because I realized I was inhaling air that had just been inside someone else. We were one giant lung drawing on the same oxygen supply.

Everyone was talking at the same time, and everyone talked louder so they could be heard. The radio was turned on but it didn't sound like a DJ. It sounded like someone just barking out syllables. I was listening hard, trying to piece the sounds together. I was thinking about my girlfriends in the front seat, laughing and moving against each other. They looked like three heads springing from one single torso. They were squirming in their seats like a litter of kittens that had just been born, and I felt sad because I wanted to be up there with them.

I was staring like this into the front seat when Steve turned around to talk to me. His body didn't move but his head spun around on his neck like a ventriloquist's mannequin, with wild eyes and big red lips. Steve's hair was long and frizzy. He said something to me then waited, like he was expecting an answer, then he talked again.

I watched his mouth, trying to catch the words as they came out, so that I could see them whole before the atmosphere screwed them up, but it didn't work. Right there, even at the tip of his lips, the words were already coming out in pieces. Steve raised one hand in the air above my head. It hovered near the roof of the car like a frightened bird. Then he brought it down and patted my head twice really fast and said, "Nice, nice."

I opened the car door and bailed out the side. A woman in the backseat with long, white hair and huge eyes like blue moonstones said, "It's not going to be any better—out there."

I went out there anyway and traced my way to the back of the car. I rubbed my fingers over the curve of the taillight. Then I raised my head and saw it up in the air—a grid like a fishnet or a web stretching across the entire sky. The web hummed and glowed with electricity, and it looked as if you could simply slip your foot through its rungs and climb it. On the top left corner was a red-white-and-blue flag with real exploding stars.

I didn't move. I heard the car door open, then close. The sound of the radio and the slam of the door were swallowed up by the blackness of the open field. Steve inched his way to me at the back of the car. He asked me how I was. I pointed up. He looked at the glowing web and nodded as if he saw it, too. He said he was sorry about getting me so high. Said he didn't know it was my first time.

I waved my hand, said I was okay, looked up at the sky again, up to those burning singing ropes, then I turned around and vomited. Steve stayed outside with me and held me from behind. He talked to me in a soft voice. He pulled my hair out of my face until I was finished.

After that night of burning ropes, I spent a lot of time with Steve, mostly driving around and talking. I suppose it's appropriate then that he would be the one to lead me finally through the beaded curtain.

Steve lived in an old warehouse downtown. It was decorated in the style of the day—a green couch with no legs in the living room, a bare mattress on the bedroom floor, the obligatory black-light room at the end of the hall, and a beaded curtain between the living room and the kitchen.

Steve had a boa constrictor named Rainbow that he had raised from just a baby. I could remember when that snake was so small that it had crawled into an eight-track player in someone's car, and we had to take the tape player apart to get Rainbow out.

But this was a few years later and Rainbow was one big, honkin' snake by now. The person sitting next to me at the party was holding Rainbow, and the snake must have smelled my perfume because he kept extending himself out, trying to land on my knee. Every time he got close I would shudder and say, "Get that thing away from me." This went on all afternoon: me, moving away from that snake.

Steve loved rock and roll. Any time you went to a party at his house, you always listened to the best and most recent music out. It was late on a Sunday afternoon—a long day of talking and laughing and drinking and smoking—when he put on a new album by Led Zeppelin. I had never really listened to this band, aside from what was on the radio. But this album was different, Steve said. It hit you like a great weight.

Before Steve put on the album, he made an announcement to the whole party that this was *the* album—you know, as if no other album had ever been made, or ever would be recorded again. This album was the last word on rock and roll. He turned the stereo up so loud the speakers rattled in the cabinets. He walked around the room telling everybody to shut up. I sat on the couch and listened because nobody could hear to talk anyway.

I listened to Robert Plant, the singer, to the way he approached a phrase from behind and swooped down on it, to the way he sang it differently each time when you were expecting to hear it again just the same way, because you heard it that way the last time through. He made it sound like an accident and so you listened because you didn't know if you would ever hear it done quite like that again. I listened to Jimmy Page play these off-balance guitar solos, giving you a feeling that you were just barely wobbling through each song with him.

I don't remember actually hearing the drums—I wouldn't *hear* drums for many years—but I do remember feeling them, the way that Bonham was in the mix, a presence, like a great, hulking machine thrashing methodically through the song. You could almost visualize him sitting there, bringing the stick down to the snare in the slowest of slow motions, keeping it from the rim just one second longer than you thought you could possibly bear. The beat could not be too slow. He had sounds to fill it.

Then this song came on and I listened like I had never listened before about the lady who was sure all that glittered was gold. I listened to the way that Plant half-missed the note and then came up from underneath, to the way he played with the listener. I heard all these things that day I had never heard before about a spirit crying for leaving.

The room slowed down. The music did not seem so loud anymore. It sounded crisp and fragile. We all sat and listened to the acoustic guitar, to the way it rang through the verses. We listened to the richness of this voice telling us the story of the stairway that lies on the whispering wind.

Then the acoustic guitars stopped and an army of electric guitars entered, ringing like church bells. They were chiming over and over on one chord, calling you to listen to this really important news. I listened to all this happen that day for the first time—the huge drum fill that crowded everybody out, the chorus of electric guitars starting up like one great engine with hundreds of spinning and whirring parts all working together to create this full, rich chord.

All these sounds—milling and stewing around each other, taking up space—suddenly split in two and step to the side for a singular voice rising slowly out of a well. It is the voice of a particular guitar trying to tell us in one singular voice everything we need to know about the stairway and about the woman.

It is at this moment, with the guitar player beginning the most orgasmic solo every recorded, that Steve Benz comes through the beaded curtain. He stands in the doorway, strands of beads streaming down his body like water, his thick red hair flying off his shoulders.

In his arms he holds an imaginary guitar, and into it he plays all of it—all the sadness we are hearing. He plays all the tragedy he has seen into that guitar with his face, with his body, with his hands.

He tells it, the sadness, truer than it's ever been told to me, and I watch. I forget everything. I forget the dirty green couch and the stale, smoky air around me. I forget the boa constrictor that is on my knee, making its way up my arm and around my shoulders.

When I finally look at that snake, I see it is nothing like what I thought it would be. It's dry and clean and strong. It climbs up my neck and hangs from my shoulders.

I touch it and talk to it, watching the way it moves— slowly with power in every cell. It anchors itself to my knee and extends out, half the length of its body. It shows me how it is possible to go far and still stay at home.

I carry that snake around the rest of the afternoon and all the rest of that night. People make jokes about my attachment to it, calling me the snake lady, calling me Medusa, calling me Eve. But I wear it anyway, with the same reverence the Sisters wear their crosses to school every day—like a woman who has made a vow with the unseen.

ACKNOWLEDGMENTS

Many thanks to the Iowa State University College of Liberal Arts and Sciences, the Hogrefe Fellowship Committee, and the Council on the Humanities for research grants that enabled this work to be completed. Thanks also to the Iowa Arts Council for their timely support.

I am grateful to the Ucross Foundation and the Ragdale Foundation for artist residencies that allowed me to complete portions of this book. A special thanks to the Writer's Voice of the Westside Y for the Capricorn Fiction Award.

Thanks are overdue to my first writing teachers at Moorhead State University: Richard DuBord, Mark Vinz, Rosemary Smith, and Alan Davis.

I am especially indebted to my editors: Robert Alexander, who significantly improved this book with his careful and insightful observations; and Bill Truesdale, a gentle reader, a mentor, and a friend.

Grateful acknowledgment is made to the editors of the magazines in which the following stories first appeared, sometimes in earlier versions.

The Crescent Review:	"Santiago's Dead"
Gargoyle:	"The Many Short Teeth of the Many Long Zippers"
The Mississippi Review:	"Do Drop Inn"
New Letters:	"Through the Beaded Curtain"
North American Review:	"Playing for the Door" and "The Movie of the World"
River City:	"The Half Life of the Note" (under the title "Naming the Beast")
Witness:	"Waiting for Dean"

"Riding through Iowa with Quest" first appeared in *Everything's a Verb* (New Rivers Press, 1995).

Debra Marquart's poetry collection, *Everything's a Verb*, was published by New Rivers Press in 1995. In the seventies and eighties, Marquart was a touring road musician with rock and heavy metal bands. She continues to perform with her jazz-poetry, rhythm-and-blues project, the Bone People, with whom she has released two CDs: *Orange Parade* and *A Regular Dervish*, a jazz-poetry companion disc to *Everything's a Verb*. An assistant professor of English at Iowa State University, Marquart is the poetry editor of *Flyway Literary Review*.